THE CHILDREN ROBBERS

or

What is Really Behind a Teacher Strike

This book is a fictional work. Any resemblance of the content to actual places and situations is purely coincidental and exists only in the mind of the reader.

By
Phillip Carl Snyder, Ph.D.

1979-375

Copyright 1979

Library Congress
Cat. Card No. 80-66622

**PUBLISHED & DISTRIBUTED
by
CUSTOM HOUSE PRESS
P. O. Box 2369
Zanesville, Ohio 43701**

All rights reserved. No part of this book may be reproduced in any form or by any means without permission in writing from the publisher.

Printed in the U.S.A.

This book is dedicated to my wife
Jo Anna Summers Snyder
for her continuing love and devotion

Extra Special Appreciation goes to:
Doral Scott Mills
and
Irene Juliet Davis Mills
for their continuing support, faith and
encouragement throughout this project

Special Credits go to:
Dorothy Stotts, my Secretary
for her understanding, typing,
and proof reading efforts

A Special Dedication is extended
to
All of the dedicated, sincere
Teachers
who are the unsung heroes
of the system.

PREFACE

This expose is being written for children who attend public schools throughout the U.S.A. Every day parents ask their children the rhetorical question, "What did you learn in school today?" The normal reply is, "I don't know." It is my contention that students at all levels through the public educational system have legitimate complaints. However, due to the lack of experience and lack of understanding of the educational process it is difficult for them to describe or explain accurately their complaints. By the same token, taxpayers and parents throughout the U.S. support their educational institutions with service and financial donations not to mention the burdens of personal and property taxes. These people also have many complaints about the educational system, however, they are not trained educators and it is difficult for them to accurately analyze the problems which they know exist. It is my hope that this book will expose some of the fallacies in the public educational system and bring to light the problems that must be solved in order to once again establish a public system of education which is both effective for the child and efficient for the taxpaying public. I have chosen the title, *The Children Robbers,* for this book because in my opinion there are many educators today who are exactly that, children robbers. These are strong words directed toward a profession that has in the past occupied a position of respect and credibility in the eyes of the public. Once again, it is my contention that respect and credibility must be earned and not taken for granted. I want it completely understood that I have no complaints with the dedicated professional educator who carries out his responsibilities both personally and professionally to the children he serves in the classroom. My only objection is to those educators who place their own personal gain, educational politics, and power hungry organizational objectives before the process of educating the child. Although these individuals represent the minority of the educational population of professionals today they are rapidly gaining control of the entire system much to the chagrin of the displeased population that they serve.

Our country is facing some of the most radical adjustments in its history. Change is a way of life and the children of the next generation must be prepared to cope with the varied and diversified responsibilities and burdens placed upon them. In order to prepare our children for the tasks that lie ahead it is essential that we expose the misuse of educational philosophies and finances in an effort to redevelop a significant public education system in the United States. Failure to do this can only result in catastrophe. Children who are not prepared to live in the future can only fail in the future. Our country and the growth of our society is based upon the values and the abilities of the citizens that we create.

Teacher's organizations in all forms are developing an organized purge on the traditional values of public education. Their selfish, short-sighted materialistic goals are undermining the entire process of the dedicated, professional, conscientious teacher. As a result, our children are being robbed of the knowledge and the abilities that they need to survive. While at the same time our parents and taxpayers are being robbed of the finances which they supply to support the systems. These organizations are a discredit to our intelligence. They must be exposed in order that our future be saved. Their survival in our system spells out the destruction of the future success of our youth. Their consistent and constant intimidation of our values undermine the total purpose of our way of life. They teach by their actions the very behaviors that the public seeks to destroy in the personality of our youth. They establish a human example of the wrong way to accomplish organizational goals. They are the epitome of a clandestine, organizational approach to the accomplishment of socialistic ideals in a democratic society. Through their misuse of organizational power and slanted political manipulation they both destroy the educational process and brainwash dedicated professional educators to rob the children in our public schools.

Once again, the overpowering influence of these organizational manipulations have not been completely felt throughout the U.S. to date. However, the educational organizations are growing rapidly and becoming more influential daily and with this influence, comes the creeping cancer of destruction which faces our educational system. One only needs to turn on a television set or pick up a newspaper to read about the strikes, threats of work stoppages, professional workdays, salary negotiations, people contact time negotiations, and other related areas of organizational pressure being misdirected toward boards of education and administrators throughout the United States. This misuse of organizationalism based upon earned reputations of past professionals represents one of the most misguided extortions ever to befall a public institution in the United States. A conspiracy within the ramifications, this misuse of public influence must be stopped.

CONTENTS

Preface VII

I. THE DISTORTION 17
Education in Past. Teachers Reputation. Favored Place in Society. Issues. Need for Organization. Demands. How Education is Controlled. Finance. New Position of Players. New Attitude of Profession. Results of Better Conditions. Personalities. Organization. Room 222 - National TV.

II. THE CRIME 50
Values Fading. Can't Read. Discipline Gone. Fair & Not Firm. No Motivation. No Dedication. Dehumanizing. Fogging Issues. Follows Examples. New is Good. Change Justifies Itself. Lack of Money Always Answer. Poor Teaching Doesn't Exist. What is Not Acceptable. Justify Don't Prove. Anything Goes -Favoritism, etc. Student Opinion. Don't Make a Wave.

III. THE GANG 86

The Organization. The Membership. Continuing Contract. Loyalty. Security. Protection. Resistant. Right. Demanding. Forceful. Professionalism. One of Many. Money. Power. Politics. Kids. Parent. Board. Administration.

IV. THE GANGSTERS 114

The Leaders - Good-Bad -Followers. Knowledgeable. Have Time. Favored Position in School. Needs Organization. Politics First and Education Second. Power Hungry. Dissatisfied. Displaced. Money not Kids. No Control. Militant. Radical. Calculating. Organized. Dishuman. Brain Washed.

V. THE HIDEOUT 142

The Teacher's Lounge. The Classroom. The School. Extra-curricular Program. Organization Meetings. The Community. Infiltrate-Central Office, Clerk's Office, Management. Board of Education. Shop-Labs, Special Programs, Music, etc. Cafeteria & Supply Rooms. Travel & Organization Meetings. Fun not Work.

VI. THE PRIZE 159

Complete Control of Public Education. Selection and Placement of Teachers. Evaluation. Salary Determination. Teaching Assignments. Number of Days. Contract Length. Pupil Contact Time. Fringe Benefits. Financial Allocations. Administration Selection. Political Control. Legal Control - State and Federal. Insurance. Retirement. Dismissal Standards. Curriculum Determination. Building Designs. Organizational Structure.

VII. THE VICTIMS 188

The Child. Less Education. More Money. Plush Surroundings. No Learning. No Supervision of Teachers. No Quality Control Over Subject Matter. Wasted Time. Meaningless Lessons. Busy Work. Poor Teacher Planning. Entertainment Not Education. Fun No Work. Freedom Not Discipline. No Respect for System. No Purpose. No Motivation. Questions Not Answers. Unfair Controls. Poor Materials. Poor Curricular Offerings. Poorly Represented. Poor Alternatives.

VIII. THE COPS 204

The School Board. Pays the Bill. Represents the People. Employs Administration. Uses the Law. Hires. Fires. Sets Salaries. Listens. Feels Pressures. Out Numbered. Slow to React. Unprepared to Cope. Poorly Equipped. Lacks Background. Lacks Facts. Infiltrated. No Security. Always Defensive. Administration - Outnumbered. Must Survive. Uses Law. Finance. Ask for Public Support. Infiltrated. Restriction Limitations. Politics. Family. Pressures, Tensions. Legal Changes. Lacks Force. Neg. Process. Loses Gracefully. Communications. Tax Payers. Normal Resentment Toward Education. Normal Administrative Functions. Parents Lose Money. Kids Lose Education. Community Loses Values. Country Loses Discipline. Nation Loses Control. Lack of Growth. Public Control Lost. Schools Lose Public Money. Teachers Lose Respect. Administrations Lose Respect. Systems Lose Reputation. Curriculum Quality. Knowledge. Achievement National Growth. Democratic System. Way of Life. Good Examples. Basic Skills. System Credibility. Teacher Confidence. Independent Thinking. Waste Money. Gradual Weakening of System. Local Control. Local Financing. Education for All.

IX. THE DISCOVERY 228

Failure of Levies. Strikes. Worker not Teacher. Labor vs. Management. Public vs. Labor. Management Survives. Public Hardens. Private Schools Emerge. Private Control. Private Finance. Children Aren't Learning. Dissatisfaction with Schools. Waste. New Releases. Increase Teacher Complaints. Fear for Children. Poor Supervision of Teachers. Lack of Discipline for Students. New Words with Little Meaning.

X. THE PUNISHMENT 244

A Destroyed Public Education System. Class Distinction in Education. Stronger Controls in Private Sector, Recruitment, Selection, Dismissal, Evaluation of Teachers. Fewer Fringe Benefits. Stranger Books. Better Informed Citizens. More Supervisory Personnel. Fewer and Weaker Contracts. More Money Controls. Better Teacher Training. Stronger Certification Requirements. Legal Controls. Abolish Negotiations. Common Salary Schedules. Better Accounting Systems.

CHAPTER I

THE DISTORTION

In the past, education in the United States has occupied a favored position in the minds of the people. We have always thought of teachers as dedicated professionals. We have looked to them as examples of our way of life. We have expected them to maintain a little higher moral character and behavior than the average man. We have trusted them with our children and we have been satisfied with the results of that trust. Some of us have been amazed to find that teachers are really human. Whenever possible we have tried to cover up the frailities of humanism which befell certain members of the profession. For example, if a teacher had a drinking problem in a community, it was hushed up quietly and that teacher was dismissed in a professional way. Not too many years ago, if a teacher married, it was considered a catastrophe and she was no longer accepted as fit for the educational profession. As a result, many teachers lived the life of a spinster with very few of the average spectator vices felt by the rest of the population. Teachers were placed upon a pedestal by the society in a credible position enjoyed by only ministers, teachers, and members of the medical profession. People not only did not want to believe bad things about educators, but they made efforts to cover up any misdoings that might have been exposed. In other words we wanted our teachers to be special and we made an effort to see to it that they were special. Because their salaries were low in the beginning it was automatic that they must be dedicated in order to teach. Therefore, little question arose about dedication. Teachers realized their favored position in the society and as a result many decided upon the profession. History books will tell us repeated incidents of favorism toward teachers in various communities. Every little community can tell you stories about teachers who were favored because of some wealthy landowner or businessman's satisfaction with the in-

THE DISTORTION

struction given his children. Stories about coaches who had winning seasons receiving gifts from local businessmen, and other harmless stories of minor corruption and favoritism toward teachers.

However, in spite of all this, teachers throughout history have been able to maintain a position of influence and credibility upon the students they serve and the society that employed them. Let's consider for a moment why this is true. One must remember that in the past teachers have usually located in one community for the duration of their professional life. This means for 10 or 20 years a teacher has lived and worked in a small community. Since our public education system involves 12 years of a student's life, 13 if one counts kindergarten, it is completely possible that a teacher might have two or three generations of offsprings from one family. Therefore, the credibility of that teacher runs deep in the community. This credibility, if used properly, is a great asset to the teacher and helps him influence the second and third generation offspring and carry out the function of education. It is a healthy situation when a teacher can be trusted and is credible and is seeking to do the work of a dedicated professional. However, when the teacher seeks to use his base or foundation to influence people to pay more taxes for less work and child manipulations, then this position of influence becomes a liability to the community. A teacher's reputation is a sacred topic of consideration. If a teacher's reputation is slandered, this can cause irreparable damage to that person as a professional and endanger his livelihood for the duration of his professional life. Therefore, one is very careful about criticizing an educator. In fact, since we are in general not trained in the process of education it is difficult to analyze how much good or how much harm is being done in the classroom to children by any particular individual. At best we can only analyze how much our child has learned or not learned as he is exposed to a particular individual during one year's time.

We all realize that teachers have many different personalities. We also understand that students will be exposed throughout life to many different personalities. We are not concerned that our children are exposed to personality con-

THE DISTORTION

flicts throughout the process of 12 years of education. We realize that this is a part of our child's growth and an expected part of the educational process. If our child, for example, is making good grades in all of his subjects except one and brings home a failing grade in that subject, we probably will pass it off after some discussion as a personality conflict. If the grade improves to a passing grade and our child survives that year, we will not give a second thought to whether or not he learned anything. In other words, it is difficult to evaluate a teacher at best and some would even say impossible.

Once again, the teacher finds himself in a favored position with regard to our society. In almost every occupation one is judged and evaluated upon the quality of his work. For example, a shoe repairman in a small community. If he does not do quality work on the shoes that he repairs, soon everyone in the community realizes that he is a poor worker. People quit coming to his shop and eventually he goes out of business. If you go to a physician time and time again, and your illness is not cured, you begin to doubt his credibility. Word circulates about his professional ability to diagnose diseases, and soon people stop making appointments with him. There are very few positions in society that completely escape evaluation. In the teaching profession it is extremely difficult because only the students really are exposed to the teachers. A teacher can have a very sincere and acceptable personality which they expose to the public. And after the classroom door is closed this can change into a very inefficient disorganized procedure for teaching. Who is to be the judge? The child is there to learn, not to judge the teacher. And the parent is not in a favored position to do this evaluation. Administrators are supposed to evaluate teachers, however, most of them at best are experts only in one or two areas of the curriculum. Therefore, for the most part teachers go unobserved and are favored with regard to the service that they perform. No one knows for sure what anyone is learning. We only know what is not being learned. The question is, "Why can't Johnny read?" This situation has continued to exist for many years in education. Over the years, teachers in communities throughout the United States have cultivated this position of

THE DISTORTION

credibility and influence in our society. At the same time they have felt that they were contributing a valuable contribution to the growth of our country. Many older teachers as they see their students graduate and become successful have felt that they contributed to the success of those students. And over the years they have felt that they were not sufficiently rewarded for their contribution. For example, if a fifth grade teacher has one of her students graduate and become a millionaire, yet she is still making her salary as a fifth grade teacher and living in the rigorous life expected by the community, she has foregone all of the pleasures or displeasures of the vices, attended church regularly, and carried out her professional responsibilities with dedication and concern. Yet, her students are more successful than she. In other words, in the minds of most experienced educators there lurks a feeling of inadequate payment by the society. They feel that they're not getting paid enough for their contribution to our way of life. They feel that they do not have the best working conditions. They feel that they deal with all of the ills of our society and yet are only paid the fees of an exalted babysitter. In other words, there is a consistent deep discontent with the financial status of the professional public educator. Teachers in general for years have been an independent, secure, and confident breed of individuals. If one analyzes why this is true, one must consider the individuals responsibilities. A teacher exists in a classroom, once he closes the door that is his world. He controls it much as a king controls a kingdom. His students are his subjects, he has influence and authority over them. He tells them what to do and how to do it and evaluates them on how well they carry it out. If they fail to carry it out, he punishes them. He issues new demands upon their time. In other words, he is Lord and Master over the subject of his classroom. He lives in his own world behind a closed door. His values are not to be judged, his ideas and philosophies are acceptable because after all, the classroom is a laboratory for the examination of all human thought. Also, we must consider that a teacher for the major part of his professional life is exposed to people with less ability than himself. His students come to him seeking his

THE DISTORTION

knowledge. It is completely conceivable that with the exception of a few bright students that his teaching ability might not be challenged. His political positions and religious values might not be questioned because there is no one to ask the questions. After a few years of this kind of situation a teacher develops confidence in his own position. Right or wrong he establishes himself in his way of doing things and right or wrong it is accepted by his subjects. Therefore, once the routine is established he is a secure individual. Challenged very rarely, if at all, and living in his own world, his classroom, doing for the most part the things that he likes and can do best. This type of situation has breeded the adage "does a teacher have 30 years experience or one years experience 30 times."

However, a few years ago this entire situation changed with the creation of the professional organization. At first professional organizations were not accepted because most teachers being the independent breed they were, could not agree with one another. In the beginning they fought with one another about all types of education methods and techniques. Each one was insecure about sharing his methods and techniques with the other for fear of peer criticism. They had been existing in their own little world for so long that they were afraid to talk about it outside of their world. Their independence led to much dissension within the educational organization and at one point failure to organize seemed inevitable.

Time passed, and as with many intangible notions, this situation healed itself. Leaders of these first educational organizations worked hard to find areas of common interest among teachers. At first they thought children and students would be an area of common interest. But after many discussions resulting in arguments about how to learn and what techniques are best for them, they gave up on children as a common area of interest. Through a trial and error method of trying to locate something which all teachers could agree upon they hit on the area of salary. This was one area where all teachers felt that they were being abused. They felt that their skills were worth more money. And they felt that the society had cheated them out of their just reward for their professional dedication. At this point in the development of professional teacher's organizations, they were probably right. For years teachers had worked for below average earnings. They had carried out all of the expectations of society and been paid a miserably low wage for their efforts. At that point in the development of teacher's organizations, teachers had a righteous just goal and reason for organizing. Their efforts were well directed. Their organization gave them needed strength. One could even say that they had found a cause which was worthy of their favored position in our society. They were going to for the first time band together in an effort to seek their just reward from the society that they had for so many years served. Their techniques were professionally sound and they approached communities earnestly seeking deserved increases in annual salary. As the various groups were successful throughout the country, more groups organized and eventually banded together in a national organization. Teachers for the first time in history realized that unity gave them strength and that strength produced results in terms of public pressure. More and more communities increased teacher's salaries. Salary schedules became a common instrument in school systems. And teachers could plan for increases on an annual basis. Indexes were arrived at and salary demands were negotiated. This was all well and good, because most of the public agreed that teachers needed increases. The public in general felt slightly guilty because they realized that they had put education low on the priority list and they realized that yes, there were teachers whom they felt had been paid poorly.

However, as teachers became successful in these salary endeavors, their success breeded new ideas. They decided if the public gave them more money than they ever expected why not new types of contracts. In the past, teachers had worked on a one year basis and if their work was unsatisfactory during any given one year period, the board of education would take it upon themselves to dismiss that teacher after a sufficient evaluation. However, a more secure arrangement had wide spread appeal among teachers. They felt if they could be contracted for many years rather than one year that they would have a more secure position in a system.

Most boards of education felt this was fair since they felt that most teachers were dedicated professionals. Here again was the carry over of the idea a few years back when teachers were originally placed upon a pedestal of respect and credibility. In fact one could even say that the first continuing contracts were probably given to teachers by students of the very teachers who received them. In other words in its original conception the continuing contract was probably not disagreeable to anyone. It gave the teacher the security of a life long position in a community while at the same time giving the community the security of having an outstanding teacher live and work in that community for the duration of his profession. Who could ask for a better situation.

It should be noted here that recently, that entire premise has been radically distorted. But more important, not only has it been radically distorted, but it has also been purposely distorted. This distortion is our major concern. Today in education, dedication to profession has been replaced by dedication to salary. Educational goals for student achievement have been replaced by organizational goals for greater power within the educational structure. Idealistic pride which at one time was the homework of a dedicated teacher has been replaced by organizational pride which stems from a militant aggressive attitude toward communities and boards of education. Teachers have turned from trying to solve educational problems to creating educational turmoil. No longer is it fashionable to suggest solutions but only to make demands upon the educational system both financially and organizationally. Weak teachers who have entered the profession seeking the higher salaries that have been obtained by the organization protect themselves by hiding behind the organizational structure and defending their existence through actuations of personal personality conflicts with administrators. As one reviews the leadership roles in many educational organizations, one finds that repeatedly teachers who have had conflicts with administrators for various reasons end up being leaders in the teacher's organization on the local level. Once they reach a position of leadership in the local organization, any further criticism voiced by an

THE DISTORTION

administrator can be rationalized as a personality conflict. Thus the teacher insures the perpetuation of his inefficiency. He has protected himself with a shield of professional organization. The public being naive about the internal workings of a school system has a difficult time differentiating between an inefficient job and a personality conflict. Thus if that teacher is dismissed, the very fact that he is an officer in the teacher's organization leaves doubt as to whether his dismissal was based upon his performance as a teacher or his performance as an organizational leader. Since many of the tactics of the teacher's organization have become militant and aggressive, even more doubt is stimulated by conflict between the board of education and the administration and a teacher who is representing the organization. The public has a difficult time differentiating between right and wrong in this situation as it exists. Since there are more teachers in the school system than there are administrators and boards of education combined, it is easier for the teacher's organization to communicate with the community at large. For example, if you have one hundred teachers in a school system, you would probably have two or three principals and a superintendent plus five board members. It is understandable that one hundred teachers can contact more people more quickly than the board of education and administration combined. Therefore, since teachers have occupied credible and favored positions in our society, people tend to listen to them especially when many of the people they are talking to are former students. They thus have a vested inside unconscious control over the influence of local population. If you have spent a school year under the direction of some teacher that possibly you were pleased with, it is difficult to imagine that three or four years after graduation if that same teacher should approach you criticizing an administrator that you had no exposure to while you were in school, which one would you be inclined to listen to? It is situations exactly like this that tend to allow the teacher organizations to gain a tremendous amount of control over local school situations. This control is planned by ex-school administrators who have taken up positions of leadership among

THE DISTORTION

the state and national teacher organizations. They are completely aware of the liability of the system. And they use the weaknesses of the system to gain strength for their organization in an attempt to gain control of the public school system. In itself this is a distortion because the public school system should be controlled by the public who elects the board of education. Teacher's organizations should be confined to professional advisement. At one point teacher's organizations were only concerned with improving salary schedules. However, today many items are points of discussion. Sick leave, maternity leave, and even paternal leave is rapidly becoming a major issue. For example, a few years ago who would ever have thought that a teacher would expect a leave paid vacation for attending his pregnant wife while the child was being born or upon the child's return to the home?

Teacher's demands are increasingly resembling the demands of unions. For example, they are demanding severance pay, grievance procedures, vacancy and transfer procedures and regulations, extended contracts and continuing contracts, some authority over the calendar of the school system, personal leave benefits, planning time, and even attempting to negotiate the time that they are in contact with students. In other words they want to work less, be in contact with students less, and be paid more. While at the same time receive greater fringe benefits in all areas, and control and regulate the curriculum, the hiring and dismissal practices and the administration of the school system.

The public takes for granted the fact that teachers are trained professionals. Four years of education does not insure expertness in teaching. For example, if your son has a history teacher, do you ever stop to think what kind of grades that teacher earned while studying history? Is it possible that your son's history teacher almost failed history himself? This is a situation known as professional credibility. When we go to a physician's office for an illness, we normally do not think of what that physician's grades were in the area of diagnosis. If we are on the operating table, we do not ask if the physician attending us received an A, a B, or a C in the techniques required of an operation. However, it's possible that in our society we should be asking questions about professional credibility. Today the taxpayer is paying a large amount of money for a good education for his children. Is it possible for children to receive a good education from people who are only interested in salary and in many cases have not adequately displayed their own expertise in the subject that they profess? This in itself is a distortion, however, it is compounded when that same individual hides behind the guides of professional organizations to hide his inability. Thus, making it difficult for administrators or supervisors to dislodge him from his lecherous position within the school system, he not only cheats the students that he serves in the classroom, but he also cheats the community of the tax dollars that they are paying to buy good education. He is able to accomplish this by using a false power base developed by the organization on the reputation of past dedicated teachers. All of these factors add up to a major distortion of public trust. That fact alone has an undermining effect upon our educational system, however, that fact compounded with the efforts that would be required to restore credibility to the system is insurmountable.

The public in its naive role has little or nothing to say about the growth of power within the system. Since they are victims of the organizational plot they can only react to the demands made by the organization. Their alternatives are all negative. If they refuse the teacher's demands and back the board of education, their children suffer from prejudice treatment from the teachers who they are exposed to as well as from poor education or no education in the cases of strikes and work stoppages. If they give in to the demands, they reinforce the teachers by giving them more money and more fringe benefits, while at the same time they reinforce the inefficiency of the system and the perpetuation of the strength of the organization. In other words if they give in they are in essence saying to the teachers we agree you deserve more money and we also agree that we do not expect you to do more work. In other words we don't care whether our children get a good education or not, we are willing to pay you what you

THE DISTORTION

demand. As you can see, both alternatives are negative and both are distortions of public trust in a public institution derived and conceived to serve the greatest possible number of children for the least amount of money. This is the distortion facing public education today.

In its original conception public education in the United States was designed to serve the greatest number of students at the least possible cost. The system was developed to be controlled on the local level by elected officials. These officials are the board of education and they are supposed to represent the thinking and the values of the community which elected them. The board of education serves as a check on how funds are spent in the school system and upon what policies govern the school system. This is right and proper because the same people that elect the board of education also live in the community and pay the taxes that support the schools. Some people criticize the board of education concept by saying that boards of education are not trained educators, therefore, they do not have the right to dictate policies governing the educational process. I strongly disagree with this position. I feel that the board of education has every right to establish the policies which govern the school system for one reason and for one reason only. That reason is that the people that they represent pay the bill for the school system. Throughout our free enterprise system every company that establishes its own policies, rules and regulations governing the money that is created by that company. It is a hallmark of our free enterprise system that the people that pay the bill control how the money is expended. This is a basic premise of our educational program. Our forefathers envisioned an educational system that would be tailored to the needs of a local situation and financed from local funds. Our educational system fulfills those requirements. It is understandable with this cost increase in education that we would see more state and federal aid to local school districts. Along with this state and federal aid we also receive more state and federal control and guidelines over educational systems. However, in most communities the board of education meeting is the last democratic threshold surviving in the community. These are public

THE DISTORTION

meetings where public officials set policies and establish control over public funds for local consumption. They resemble New England town meetings where people may attend and voice their objections and criticisms as well as their compliments upon the makeup of the system. They are truly democratically conceived and legally sound methods of controlling a school system. Most school board members are permanent residents and taxpayers within the school system that they serve. Therefore, they are closely in touch with the people that that system serves and understand the value system and the political structure of the community that is involved. In essence they are the best prepared to lend leadership to the development of a consistent set of values for the students that are the products of the system. They deserve to have control over the policy making procedure existing within the organization. A teacher's organization cannot logically control the finances of a school system. They have a vested interest in higher salaries and greater fringe benefits. They also have a vested interest in inefficient management of operational funds within the school system. The poorer the management of the funds for the spending efficiencies, the more money that is available for more salaries and more fringe benefits. Therefore, it is illogical that a teacher's organization should control tax money which represents public funds for use for public education. However, this is exactly the goal of most teacher's organizations.

At one point in our history the board of education had complete control of the school system. They hired a professionally trained educator as an administrator and instructed him on how to administer the school system in line with the communities values and goals for education. The administrator in turn carried out the wishes of the board and administered the school system consistently with the policies established by the board. The teachers organization stressed the professional development of teachers. Teachers were employed by the administration and board of education to teach the various subject matter areas where their expertise existed. All of this organization has radically changed.

Today boards of education are being cast in ineffective roles. Teachers

THE DISTORTION

organizations are gaining more power over the school system. The only barrier which exists between teachers organizations gaining complete control of the school system are the administrators who are holding hard lines against teacher organization control and boards of education who are willing to fight against a creeping organizational strength of the teachers. Remember almost everyone in the school system is a member of the teachers organization or the non-certified organization which involves the custodians, bus drivers, and cafeteria workers.

Another term for teachers organization would be teachers union. Teachers do not like to be classified as union workers because they desire a professional image. However, the tactics used by the teachers organization are identical to the tactics used by hard core unions throughout the country. In essence, the only people who are not members of the teachers union or of a union within the school system are the administrators and the board of education. Since the union workers, the teachers, and the cafeteria workers, custodians, and bus drivers are all unionized employees of the school system they are all seeking the same basic demands. Increased salaries and increased fringe benefits as well as increased control over the organization, supervision, and evaluation of the school system. The only people in the school system working against this type of biased control are the board of education and administration. The board of education, of course, is a part time organization which usually meets on a monthly basis to discuss school issues. On a daily basis the only resistance to total teacher control school system is the administration. The administration is vastly out numbered by the teachers within the school system. As was indicated before, many of the leaders of the teachers organization are people within the school system that have time on their hands. For example, a shop teacher who puts the boys to work on various projects and leaves his classroom to talk with other teachers in the hallways and in their classrooms about organizational matters. Or a distributive education teacher who spends one and one-half hours a day in class and spends the rest of his day driving around the community to various businesses seeking jobs for students. It

THE DISTORTION

has been called to my attention that from time to time these types of people take on leadership positions within the organization. They, thus, use their unscheduled time in the classroom to carry out functions of the organization. This kind of activity makes it increasingly difficult for the administration to supervise the school system. While at the same time if the administration criticizes these individuals for their inefficiencies, these people will claim that the administration has a personality bias and that he is in effect not criticizing their work but criticizing them as individuals. The result of this kind of manipulation and undermining within the school system is a poor education for boys and girls and an ineffective board of education and administration. Rules and regulations for dismissing teachers are becoming increasingly difficult. As the membership of teachers organizations or teachers unions increase, these organizations have more money to put into legal lobbying and also legal counsel which makes it more difficult for an administrator to dismiss a teacher. If, for example, an administrator attempts to provide a negative evaluation of a teacher's performance and dismiss the teacher, he has repeatedly in many situations found himself in court with a lawsuit against him. The lawsuit is financed by the teachers organization. Thus, it makes it easy for a teacher to hide behind the organization and defend his inefficiency and his ineffectiveness in the classroom. The threat of a lawsuit constantly hangs over the board of education and the administration. Thus, making them ineffective in the supervision and evaluation of teachers and almost completely ineffective in teacher dismissal. This guarantees the teacher not only a contract, a job, and a secure position within the school system, but also the continuation of the perpetuation of the organization as well as regularly scheduled increases in salary and fringe benefits. All in all it is a very lop-sided situation in favor of undeserving teachers organization within the school system. Each year boards of education spend more and more money seeking legal advice in an attempt to combat the creeping infiltration of teachers organizations. They ask administrators to improve evaluating techniques and make an effort toward the dismissal of certain

THE DISTORTION

proven ineffective teachers. All of these efforts are in vain since the organizations are growing faster and have more funds available every year for the perpetuation of their distortion. The public becomes increasingly misinformed since these organizations also carry on a continuous public relations program selling the traditional ideals and dedication of teachers. The public is always vulnerable to hearing a credible story about a dedicated teacher. These stories are being manufactured and perpetuated by teacher organizations under the false pretense of dedication and professionalism. The main goal remains increase salaries, increase fringe benefits, and additional control over the functioning of the school system. Which all leads to a vested interest in control over public funds without public representation.

In order to completely understand the distortion of our present system of education, one must not only understand the goals of the teachers organization, but also the strategy that they employ to accomplish these goals. These organizations are national in scope and represent a large amount of money and concentration. They are highly organized by well-trained professionals in the art of subterfuge and deception. Their final goal is complete control over their own destiny as professional educations. Meaning that not only will they control the salary schedules and the fringe benefits, but also the placement of their own people, the evaluation of their own people, and the dismissal of their own people. In other words they are attempting to rob the public of control over their own tax dollars as it is applied to the education of their children. They are not doing this by chance, but by plan. There is a popular television program featuring incidents within the school system sponsored by one of these organizations. Many people watch this television program on nationwide television every week. If one studies the programming carefully, one will see that the teacher is always right. The administration is played up as necessary but not essential as a part of the school system. And one never really evidences any importance to the board of education. In other words, this is an attempt on a national level to continue to perpetuate the myth that all teachers are dedicated professionals working toward the best possi-

THE DISTORTION

ble education for boys and girls. At one point in the development of our education system it is possible that this premise would apply to the majority of teachers. However, today it is my contention that this is a premise which is falsely conceived and deviously perpetuated by the organization which represents self-centered teachers who are striving to demand control which they have no legal right to.

We have discussed many strong statements regarding teachers organizations within the United States today. It should be mentioned that we are talking only about strong organizational type teachers. There are still many dedicated teachers who are working for the good of boys and girls. However, they are rapidly becoming outnumbered by young and old organizational types who are striving to accomplish devious ends. Our concern lies with maintaining control of the school system with the board of education and administration as it was legally and rightly conceived historically within our system. We are also concerned with maintaining quality education within the classroom. We feel that the only way that quality education can be maintained is with an effective continuous evaluation and dismissal procedure. If poor teachers are not weeded out of our system and if poor instruction goes unnoticed, then the gradual effect on our system can be nothing more than negative. Since the welfare of our community and our nation depends upon the preparedness of our youth, it is essential that we establish a credible way of maintaining quality education within our schools. It becomes paramount that we communicate nationally the creeping unionistic control over the minds of our children. While at the same time constantly and consistently watch how funds are expended toward the accomplishment of our goal of national education. Boards of education and administrators must be supported by the public in order to offset the strategy of these unionistic organizations. The only power base which is large enough to nullify the strength of these organizations lies with the taxpayers. The board of education is only as strong as the taxpaying public which elects it and backs it in crisis situations. If a strike or other pressure tactics are used to try to pressure

THE DISTORTION 49

your board of education into submission to salary demands, public support must prevail. It is impossible for the board of education, the administration, and the school system to survive without the continued conscientious support of the taxpaying public as a buffer to the gaining influence of unionistic teachers organizations.

CHAPTER II

THE CRIME

The crime teachers are committing by participating and supporting teachers organizations is extremely complicated. In some cases teachers are innocently being manipulated by the political structure of the teachers organization. They are aware of the strategy and the goals of the parent organization and are used as pawns in the giant power struggle for control of the school system. The effect of their crime is devastating, students are being robbed of their education. They are being used to gain political ends for the organization. While at the same time, parents and taxpayers are being influenced by the teachers through the students and the taxpayers are being robbed of the money that they pay for a quality education. The ramifications of these principles are endless.

Teachers in the organization use

THE CRIME

classroom time to discuss heated political issues in the community with the students during class. These students then carry home the opinions of their teachers and plant these opinions with their parents. The parents being naive about what is going on in the school situation listen to the students and assume that the stories they hear are true. Therefore, many parents support the contentions of the teachers because they are influenced by their own sons and daughters. At the same time these teachers are being paid by the very taxpayers who are supporting them. They are being paid to educate the children not to use them as a way to gain political end in the community.

This can be better understood if one considers the fact that people in the United States are under the control of teachers for twelve years of their public education. During these twelve years they learn to respect teachers and value their opinions. As the system stands now, the thirteenth year, those same students who have been under the influence and control of these teachers are asked to vote for tax levies and support salary increases for teachers in the community. Every time an additional tax levy passes the money is negotiated into teachers salaries by force through the teachers organization. At the same time the teachers who are negotiating the salary increases, in other words robbing the tax dollar from the pocket of the taxpayer and using the school system and the children as justification for increasing salaries beyond reasonable limits, manipulate student opinion and a naive taxpaying public into supporting their cause. Because of the majority number of teachers in a school system it is easy for them to influence the community toward thinking their cause is just. As a result, taxes go up and up and school systems do not improve. Because every dollar that comes into the school system is immediately siphoned off into teacher salary increases and in no way improves the educational process for the child. The school systems provide poorer and poorer education while cost goes up and up and teachers improve their situation by teaching less and less subject matter in the classroom and earning more dollars for it. These same teachers realize that if they can make students happy while they are ex-

THE CRIME

posed to them, that the chances are that these students will support them after they graduate. Therefore, they become more lenient in their attitude toward students and allow all types of uneducational activities to take place in the classroom. The students, of course, do not tell their parents this because the students enjoy the new freedom that they have as a result of the teacher's leniency. The teacher enjoys the freedom because he no longer has to plan nor require learning in his classroom. The parent is naive because all he hears is that everything is fine in the school and that his child likes the teachers that they have. The disheartening fact about the entire situation is that students are not learning, teachers are not teaching, taxpayers are paying more money, and boards of education and administration are left in the position of trying to explain why education is not improving in the school system, why teachers leave the building before students, why discipline is poor, and why there is conflict in the school system about salary increases. Since the public generally wants peace in the family and a cooperative attitude in the schools, it becomes an impossible task for the board of education and administration to continue to have discipline and good education while at the same time suffering from the demands of teachers organizations and the lack of support from the public. All of this adds up to a crime against humanity and our way of life.

To understand the complexities of the problem, let us look at our value system. Over the past three years the traditional values of our way of life have been fading. In order to understand the implications of this fact, one must think of how he arrived at his way of thinking originally. In the last generation, values were taught in the home as well as in the school. Parents reinforced these values as well as teachers and other symbols of authority in our society. Today values are fading. Teachers no longer require discipline or teach discipline as part of the curriculum. It is fashionable to be strict and to be organized in the classroom. This type of philosophy is perpetuated by the teachers organization by rationalizing it under new educational terms. Some teachers call it individualizing instruction. Another way of explaining this is to simply say that each student may do what he

THE CRIME

likes, when he likes, how he likes within the school system. The open school concept is another liberalizing method of instruction. Many teachers interpret this to mean that students may go where they like when they like and do what they like within the school. The abolishment of dress codes means that students may wear what they like when they like where they like. All of these concepts are highly liberal and anti-discipline. The dual standard is fading in the schools. At one time preference was given to age and experience. A teacher because he was older was allowed to smoke in a set aside lounge in the school. Some teachers would go to the boiler room to have a cigarette between classes. Today the dual standard has been abolished since teachers can smoke in the schools, students feel that they should be able to smoke also. So therefore, many of them do. They are able to do this because teachers do nothing about it. In a high school of three thousand students there are only two or three administrators. If the teachers do not help enforce the discipline within the school, there is no discipline. And because of the new liberalized way of approaching education, many teachers will not go into the halls while the students are changing classes. They turn their head when they see discipline problems and they refuse to recognize their responsibility for the students that they are supposed to be teaching. All of these things represent more work and more effort on the teacher's part. Many of todays teachers are interested only in salary and not in students. They work for the money and they do as little as possible, and they spend what time they are in school dedicated to the political goals of the organization and the influence of students toward their support.

This is primarily why when Johnny comes home he can not read. Discipline is old fashioned and education of children takes a second priority to the political manipulation of the community in favor of dollar increases and shorter working hours. The old dedicated image of the teacher who required Johnny to stay after school and study his spelling lesson has been replaced by a liberal looking, liberal acting, pro-education association, union type individual who is only interested in drawing a high salary and decreasing his

THE CRIME

working hours within the school. He is in most cases more interested in educational politics than in the educational process. His idea of a good teacher is one who takes his one or two days sick leave each month on a regular basis whether he is sick or not, forces the board of education to pay the highest possible salary the school system can afford regardless of the consequences to the educational process, is able to negotiate a contract with the board of education which will limit his contact time with pupils, manipulates himself into a position within the school system which gives him free time to work on organizational problems, presents a liberal image to the students and sympathizes with their demands upon the establishment and the system. In general, they are renegades and descenders with regard to the normal traditional process of education. This is the individual that throws a temper tantrum in the form of a strike when he doesn't get his own way with the board of education. Who lets air out of the bus tires and damages the brake lines in order to get a salary increase. Disrupts the educational process during the school year in order to force the board of education to pay his price. Uses the media in the form of the radio, television, and newspaper to perpetuate the false image of a dedicated professional. While at the same time does everything possible to discredit the administration and the board of education in the eyes of the taxpaying public. This is the individual who we are trusting the future of our country and the livelihood and education of our youth. Is it any wonder that with this image to follow that open demonstration and student dissent is a national pastime in our country today. How can you expect students to cut their hair and discipline their personalities when their teachers won't. One may ask, how are these times perpetuated in the school and what are the details and everyday incidents which contribute to this type of atmosphere? For example, we might consider a traditional approach to discipline. Teachers have long been taught that one should be firm as well as fair in dealing with students. Today that philosophy is considered old fashioned and has been replaced with an attitude of favoritism and laxity. For example, students in the community who have influential parents are treated fair.

While at the same time these same influential students are given preferential treatment in the classroom. Very little work is required of them and in some cases they are given leadership positions over other students. Thus, a pecking order is formed within the classroom based upon teacher favoritism. Certain students from certain families get the good grades and other students from less influential families are given poor grades. Little or none of this is based upon the actual achievement of the student. Since grading is subjective to begin with, it is very easy for a teacher to justify any grade that he gives any student. The only recourse is that the student will complain and eventually drag the parent into the situation. As a result, teachers give very few poor grades. Thus, eliminating any parental complaints. In other words, they pass everybody regardless of what they know or what they learn. While at the same time favoring the influential families over the poor families or less influential families in the community. These teacher organization types do little or nothing to motivate students. Their only contribution to motivation lies in the fact that they are liberal in image and appeal to the students in popularity. By being popular with the students they take on the role of a peer or friend and motivate students out of a mutual friendship rather than a teacher-student relationship. They justify this behavior by saying they are relating to the students. In other words, they feel that communication on a popularity level is better than discipline as a means of motivation. As a result, the students who like them work for them and support them as teachers. The students who do not like them or have personality conflicts seek out other teachers who have compatible personalities and support them. All of this supports the contention that there no longer exists an order of behavior within the school system. In general, among this new breed of teachers, anything one can get away with is acceptable. Over-familiarization with students is commonplace among the new breed. A dehumanizing popularity approach to education is fashionable. The development and perpetuation of knowledge has taken a second seat to an active political approach to the classroom. Dedication has been replaced by a machinelike union

THE CRIME

type teacher who is interested only in money and fringe benefits. Lack of exposure to students is considered a fringe benefit. The ideal situation for many of the new breed is one in which they have very few or no students to deal with. All of this adds up to a poor education for children. Students are confused because the value systems that they learn from their parents are radically different from the value systems perpetuated by their teachers.

I have been involved in situations where teachers have used students to place political pressure on the board of education and administration. They do this by developing friendships with the students and using class time to explain their political goals to the students. They then encourage the students to organize in their favor and perpetuate their popularity in the community. These students then carry the message that the teacher perpetuates to their parents and the parents in turn show up at a board meeting many times accompanied by the students themselves to support a teacher who is undeserving. The board of education and administration at that point look like the bad guys.

As a result, it is difficult and in some cases impossible to dismiss a poor teacher because of his political support from a naive community. I have seen situations where teachers did absolutely nothing with regard to education. But because the students like them and the students told their parents that they like them, these teachers use the students to protect their job and their position. A naive public must become aware of the internal workings of their school system. This situation can only be corrected by a well informed public who is willing to recognize political manipulation as it is perpetuated by this new breed of teachers. Since this type of misbehavior is unheard of in educational circles, it is difficult to realize its significance and impact upon the educational system as a whole. Yet, it is my contention that every school system has at least one element of this type working slowly and methodically to gain control of the minds of the children and the dollars of its taxpayers. These individuals consistently slant issues and confuse political positions in an effort to influence the minds of students and the taxpaying public toward their unjust goals. The

THE CRIME

same teachers who dehumanize the educational process and insult the integrity of the common man replace learning in the classroom with political influence. Every decision which comes out of the central office or from the board of education is twisted and manipulated into a malicious attempt to punish teachers. Students are led to believe that administrations and boards of education are bad and only strive to discredit the educational process. While at the same time, they are told that teachers are good and are trying to develop the educational process. Teachers reinforce this belief with students by being popular with them and letting them have their way in the classroom. In other words, students are constantly exposed to negative comments about the political issues within the school system. These issues range from such things as increased salaries to shorter school days and even involve personality. I have known for example teachers who received evaluations from principals and administrators on their teaching performance who would actually post these evaluations on the bulletin board in classroom and discuss them openly with the students. Of course, their discussions were biased and in this way they were able to cast the administration as a negative thinking, narrow-minded authority trying to discredit them as good teachers. Of course, what they do not realize is that these biased attempts toward prejudicing the minds of students generates its own conclusion. I have found that most of the new breed will stop at nothing to gain their ends. There are no areas remaining in the educational process which are not vulnerable to criticism and distortion from the union oriented teacher. Issues are always distorted and manipulated in a way to make the teacher and the teachers organization look right and the administration and the board of education look wrong. These teachers through their rebellious attitude and political falsities are able to promote their own welfare within the school system. Students learn from them how to dissent, criticize, organize, and demonstrate against the rules and regulations of the system. They learn from them the character and the manner of an aggressive militant liberal faction of our society. They are trained by the image set by the teachers how to accomplish their goals of change within the system by demonstration and pressure politics. These individuals call themselves teachers. In my opinion, at best they are politically oriented, dehumanized, union-like parasites living upon the minds of our youth and the pocketbooks of our public.

They perpetuate their myths by claiming anything new is good. They emphasize that change justifies itself. By perpetuating these liberal concepts they condition the minds of their students to be receptive of their disruptive and bias opinion toward the establishment and the system. They claim to present both sides of issues while at the same time rob the students of an unbias presentation of controversial issues. They represent only themselves and their own purposes while claiming to be educators. They are an insult to the profession and to the public that they serve. They are biased, contemptible, calculating, and represent an uncontrolled threat to the system which employs them. They are constantly destroying the traditional values and goals of our educational system while at the same time replacing these traditional values with biased opinions and directions of their educational organization. They are striving to rob the community of its educational integrity and use its limited resources for their own personal gain. They are committing the crime of distorting the minds of youth in the name of education. They are using their learned abilities to manipulate public thinking. They are discrediting the traditional institution of the teacher and replacing it with a biased self-centered political manipulator. They are using a combination of intellect and money to that end.

Teachers organizations constantly claim that lack of money is the basic cause of all problems facing the school district. It is my contention that this belief is utterly false. As we all well know, money is a central problem to any of us if we do not have it. However, most school systems have sufficient operating budgets until the demand of the teachers organization for salary increases becomes so excessive that they drain the funds that would normally be used to buy textbooks, run buses, operate cafeterias, and maintain buildings. So you see, lack of money is a problem in school operations since they are funded through public taxation. But it

THE CRIME

is a problem that would be greatly reduced if teachers would accept progressive increases in salary according to the money provided by the taxpaying public. Boards of education and administrators have for years approached the public with increased demands for greater taxation. Legislators have provided for additional state aid and in general every effort has been made to provide school systems with the amount of funds needed to operate. In many cases these funds never influence the education of children. This results because they are siphoned off by the teachers organization in the form of salary increases. Most boards of education are understanding and are willing to grant salary increases within the financial ability of the system. However, when the demand becomes so radical and so emphatic that they cannot be ignored, boards of education and administrators are forced to drain money from other priorities within the school system to pacify the teachers demands. These temper tantrums of the new breed of political educators are causing the very basic financial problems of the school district and in many cases making it impossible to operate. Most school systems have annual salary increases which are a part of a master salary index. The negotiation process perpetuated by the teacher organization require financial increases beyond those which are automatically given. This means that teachers receive not only the annual increase offered by the board of education which has been a planned part of the budget, but they also want an additional increase which is negotiated on an annual basis and for which no funds have been budgeted. If boards of education refuse to submit to these excessive demands, the teachers organization returns with a threat of strike. This forces the board of education to either go out and ask the taxpaying public for additional funds in order to pacify the teachers, or borrow money on anticipated revenue generated by taxes during the next school year and pay the teachers their excessive demands out of these funds. Either method of satisfying teacher demands is unacceptable to the taxpaying public and irresponsible financial management by the board of education and the administration. The alternative remains a teacher's strike or work stoppage and the effect of that is a degeneration of the educational process. If the board of education chooses to fight, they only hurt the children who lose the education that they would normally be receiving during the strike period. Thus, it is basically impossible for the board of education and administration to win in a situation where excessive demands by an organized politically oriented teachers group have been instigated.

It has long been a contention of teachers organizations that salary increases are deserved for additional years of experience. This means, in general, that a teacher who has taught two years is a better teacher than one who has taught one year. This thought has been continued to mean that a teacher who has taught fourteen years is a better teacher and deserves a greater salary than a teacher who has taught five years. Many educators have disputed the validity of such a contention. However, it remains a fact that most teachers are working on fixed salary increases which automatically guarantee them salary increases each year for a set number of years service. One thought that has surrounded this issue has been the question whether or not a teacher who has taught fourteen years really has fourteen years of experience or one year of experience fourteen times. If for example, a teacher who has taught fourteen years has one year of experience fourteen times, then does that teacher deserve fourteen increases in salary during that span of time. If that teacher does not deserve these increases, then why should boards of education be tied to fixed salary indexes which mandate that that teacher will receive these indexes on a yearly basis. This points out a recommendation which has often been made that teachers should be paid on a merit system. Most business positions are rewarded by merit increases. Those people doing the best job get the greatest increase and those people doing the poorest job get less increases. However, in the teaching business the problem is that the results of a good teacher are intangible. If a teacher does his job well, a change in the behavior of the child is evidenced. In other words, the child has learned. However, how do you measure how much a child has learned in a particular class as a result of exposure to a particular teacher. This has been an age old problem in education and to this day has not been satisfied to the extent that merit increases are successful.

Since evaluation of teachers performance has traditionally been a difficult problem for educators to overcome, teachers have taken advantage of the situation. In other words, it becomes a subjective judgement as to whether teacher A is better than teacher B with regard to teaching English. Unless one or the other teacher has obvious difficulty handling students or obvious organizational problems, it is extremely difficult to differentiate between their effectiveness with regard to the presentation of their subject matter specialization. Each teacher is trained or specialized in a particular area of the curriculum. However, who in the school system is qualified to evaluate all areas of the curriculum with equal expertise. This job usually falls into the hands of a supervisor or the principal. Neither of these individuals are fully qualified to evaluate the extremes of the curriculum represented by all the teachers who serve them. For example, a principal may specialize in business education yet he is placed in a position where he must evaluate a physics teacher or a calculus teacher while at the same time an English instructor and possibly an art or music teacher. As you can see, by using a poorly qualified individual to make a detailed evaluation of the success of a particular specialized teacher is almost a virtual impossibility. Teachers organizations realize the difficulty involved in successfully evaluating teachers and as a result they claim that all evaluations made by administrators are poor. If a teacher is given a poor evaluation by an administrator, the teachers organization immediately claims that there is a personality conflict. Basically, most people understand personality conflicts better than they understand teacher performance. Thus, a teacher who can establish that a principal is giving her a poor evaluation because of a personality conflict, thus gains a position such as political immunity. In other words, the more negative things that the principal says the more it appears there is a personality conflict and the more it appears that the teacher is unjustifiably reprimanded. All of these things lead to poor teaching in the classroom. Teachers are not properly supervised nor properly evaluated. When they are evaluated poorly, they hide behind the personality aspects of the evaluation and they gain a position of political immunity from which to launch political attacks upon the school board and administration. At the same time they use students in the classroom while they are employed by the taxpayers to instigate political uprisings in the community. Their organization forces the board of education to pay higher salaries for less teaching and students receive less education. Teachers thus complete the circle of political intrigue by gaining a position of continuing contract within the school system and job security for life. Laws make it virtually impossible to dismiss a teacher for less than gross immorality or malfeasance and these are extremely difficult charges to prove. Teachers once again find themselves in a favorite position within our society. They are getting more money, working less, laboring under less supervision, using students for their own political purposes, squeezing money from the taxpaying public, placing undue political pressure upon the board of education and administration, making excessive demands upon the school system and the community that they serve, and doing all of this in the name of public education. Their crime is the crime of using their learned intelligence to take advantage of students on the individual level, the community on the group level, and the taxpaying public on the financial level. They justify their existence and their ineffectiveness in the classroom by claiming that these are characteristics of a new process of education. They use standardized tests which are based upon national norms to evaluate the progress of students. They then justify their ineffectiveness with the results from nationalized tests which have involved students from other school districts being taught by this same type of teacher. The overall effect of this approach to education is degrading and insulting to our way of life. Once under the protection of the teachers organization teachers are free to develop their own existence within the school system. In many cases they run private businesses using public funds and student labor. For example, a shop teacher might have private projects going for people in the community which he is being paid for while at the

THE CRIME

same time he is using school materials and student labor to accomplish them. An automotive shop might repair automobiles, paint them, or repair engines and the teacher receives a fee in the terms of a kickback and use school purchased parts to repair the engines and student labor to do the work. In one instance a teacher repaired refrigerators in a shop in a school district and actually carried on a private business while using public funds. In the process of taking advantage of the public, teachers also use their specialized knowledge to take advantage of and manipulate board of education members. Since most of the officers in the teachers organization at the state and national level are ex-superintendents and ex-school administrators, they realize the weaknesses in our board of education structure. Since they know that board of education members have no specialized knowledge about education, they realize their insecurity when dealing with teachers. Teachers play upon this insecurity and use the lack of knowledge of board members as a method of infiltrating boards of education and splitting or weakening them. If, for example, a board of education is made up of five members and all at once one member is favoring every proposal made by the teachers organization, the following political intrigue mounts. First, the administration is discredited because the board of education member who is sympathizing with the teachers organization publicly questions various proposals made by the administration. Secondly, the teachers organization brings in groups of people so that the board of education member who is making a public display will have an audience to support him. If he is a politically minded individual, he may feel that by catering to the audience before him he is able to insure his re-election as a board of education member. While at the same time he gains support from the teachers in the school system by supporting their point of view. Since it is a weakness in our society that the majority usually fails to speak out, he becomes a spokesman for the minority. Thus, in this situation the minority represents the teachers organization, they will eventually gain their ends because the rest of the board of education must satisfy the majority and keep peace in the school system. By constantly playing this deranged game of political manipulation, teachers organizations are able to split boards of education, manipulate public opinion, and siphon off all existing funds into salary increases and fringe benefits. Once again, this adds up to a crime against the educational process and flagrant distortion of the traditional image of teacher dedication.

Today this crime against children is even deeper. Teachers no longer feel the compulsion to present factual subject matter or accurately represent both sides of controversial issues. Instead they would rather justify each controversial issue from the position of their organization. In other words, student's minds are manipulated in the classroom. Teachers use students to justify their own position and to gain political support in number within the school system. It is no longer important what is right or wrong, but rather who has the majority opinion of those people associated directly with the school system. Teacher organization leaders feel if they can sway the political positions of the board of education and the community by using their popularity with students to show support for programs and salary increases that their position is justified. They are no longer concerned with the morality of the issue but rather with the practical monetary benefits derived from their actions. As a result of this mob philosophy toward education, teachers organizations use every conceivable type of manipulatory technique. Some students are threatened by grades and tentative devices in order to gain their support. At the same time, other students are shown favoritism and given positions of authority within the classroom in order to enjoin their leadership and support for teacher causes. Among the new breed teachers social structures develop with authority and responsibility delegation attached within each classroom. Each new breed teacher has his own "pets". These students have been identified on the basis of personality compatability with the teacher. Once the teacher identifies these students who have a natural radical flair toward the establishment, he then delegates authority to these individuals and sets up a chain of command within the classroom structure. Although these students are not learning

THE CRIME

the subject matter which should be taught in the classroom, they are taking part in the political issues existing within the school. These students are usually favored by giving them assignments to work for the cause which currently is being perpetuated by the teacher organization. They are ensured good grades by the teacher and are favored in every aspect of the school situation. Many times they are friendly with the teachers outside the school and visit the homes of the teachers for work sessions concerning the various issues relating to the operation of the school. Most students in this category are of high school age since they are more aware of the political manipulation within the school such as dress code violations, busing regulations, and other disciplinary and establishment-oriented rules and regulations. Once again, the crime which exists here is the fact that teachers are not supporting boards of education, but instead are supporting students in a militant stand toward rules and regulations established for the operation of the school system. At the same time, these new breed teachers are using students to perpetuate the desires of their teachers organization while robbing these same students of the natural educational process. They are accomplishing this under the disguise of using these students as student helpers or student aids. The student is basically naive as to what is happening to him. He only realizes that he is in a favored position with his teacher and that he does not have to work hard to graduate from high school. These two factors are motivation enough for him to participate in this intrigue. The pressures of the normal school operation are lifted and the student is free to wander the halls and carry out the commands of his teacher with regard to the perpetuation of the teachers organization's political position on current issues within the school system. All of this adds up to a distortion of the educational process. The student is robbed of his education and thus carries nothing with him from one year to the next regarding the subject matter which should be covered in these situations. In some instances, subject matter is brushed over and covered lightly in order to justify the situation. Whenever supervisory controls such as principal's evaluations are perpetuated, the scene changes and teachers emphasize subject matter. In some cases they even condition students to the fact that a principal is going to be present and ask them to play the role of a student for a short period of time in order to get the administration off their back. Teachers in some cases use students to set up a situation which looks like a normal classroom in order that their evaluations by the principals are accurate and acceptable. Here again, it is impossible for a principal with fifty or sixty teachers under his supervision to properly evaluate and control them. In the past the public has had confidence in the professionalism of teachers and close supervision and evaluation was not essential. However, the new breed of teachers is taking advantage of this situation and using the laxity in evaluative and supervisory systems to set up and manipulate student opinion with regard to current political issues. Students who resist this manipulation or criticize teachers for their opinions regarding boards of education and administration are penalized by threats of poor grades and by heavy work loads. As their resistance becomes more intensified, they are faced with threats of failure and outcast by other members of their class who support the teacher's position. The psychological relationship between a teacher and a student has always been one of respect and admiration. Thus teachers have a natural platform from which to launch their influence upon the minds of students. This collation between new breed teachers and militant students eliminates discipline problems for the teacher, heightens a popularity status for what would otherwise be an unpopular teacher and develop a pleasant environment for the teacher to work with the students of his choice. At the same time it eliminates work from the educational process on the part of the student, and guarantees the student that he is accepted by the teacher and will receive good grades for his contribution to the process. Thus, from the surface or to the outsider, the situation looks content. Students are happy with teachers and teachers are happy with students and both teachers and students are unhappy with boards of education and administrators. The public then asks the question, "why are the teachers unhappy with the board of education?". Could it be that we have the

THE CRIME

wrong board of education? They in turn start looking for new board members. The public is unaware that the teachers have certain selected people in the community that they are pushing for board election. The public in their search for new board members might because of the influence and political campaigning of the teachers elect to the board several members who represent teacher opinion. If this happens in a community, the school system is out of control because there will be no conflicts. Teachers will be happy, students will be happy, and the Board of Education will be happy, however, no education will be taking place. The educational process will have been replaced with a political oriented teachers organization who is interested in high salaries and better working conditions along with less responsibility. They will perpetuate their organization by fighting with students on major issues and by electing their own board of education members who in turn will pick administrators who will side with teachers on critical issues and eliminate all conflict within the school system. Once again, a peaceful school system is not a sign of a good school system. It could in many cases very well be the sign of a school system which is completely under control of the teachers organization and in turn not doing an adequate job of education. Once the organization gains complete control of the school system it is nearly impossible to regain control. Thus, taxes begin to rise as teachers gain more and more salary increases, the tax paying public must pay more and more for their services. Educational quality dwindles. Since there are no longer effective administrative and supervisory evaluations teachers are their own bosses. This results in a laxity and in some cases complete rejection of traditional educational processes. School becomes a game and every day a party. Students and teachers spend their year doing things that are fun. No education results. The community loses because the children are not given a basic public education and are not prepared upon graduation to assume their position of responsible citizens. A "don't make a wave" attitude exists throughout the school system. The major crime of the deterioration of our public educational process has been committed. All of those involved are content with the exception of the public who is completely unaware of what is happening. As the cost of education goes up and the quality of education goes down, the public is left paying the bill.

CHAPTER III

THE GANG

Today many local teachers organizations have gained a gang mentality toward the problems of education. They roam the halls much in the same manner as neighborhood gangs roamed the streets and alleys of the ghettos. They seek out conflicts with the administration. They seize upon every slight interpretation of board policy in an attempt to develop conflict over it. They protect their members by secrecy and concealment. They allow any position to be justified by the teachers organization as long as it protects all members of the gang.

This gang mentality manifests itself in many ways throughout the school system. Some members refuse to talk directly with administrators. All members conceal information regarding the operation of the school system from the administration and the board. The gang has a self appointed structural hierarchy. The leaders plan the strategy and the attacks. While many of the members are followers and merely participating in a passive way when the battle begins. All members are expected to feed any undesirable information to the authority figures. All members are constantly gathering information throughout the school system. They attempt to infiltrate all areas of the school and community. They carry back information to the hierarchy and this information is then added to the strategy with regard to individual situations. For example, if a teacher is doing a poor job in a community and there are many complaints about this teacher, every teacher who hears a complaint carries this complaint back to the president of the teachers organization, in turn the person making the complaint is reported to the organization and the organization makes attempts to start rumors to combat the complaint. In some cases the organization starts rumors to discredit the complaintant. In other cases teachers use political tactics to discredit the student of the parent who is complaining. In other words the threat of poor grades and failure. All secretaries throughout the school system are probed constantly to find any new information concerning the direction of the Board of Education and Administration. If new monies come into the system, the State organization reports this to the local gang. The gang then sets about to figure out strategies which will allow them to get pay increases. The basic strategy is to constantly keep pressure upon the administration and board of education so that it is impossible for them to take an offensive stature. All of this contributes to a very tight organization within the teacher ranks. The new breed militant teacher thrives on conflict with the administration and board of education. His desire is to gain as much power over the direction of the school system and the financial spendings as possible. In this pursuit all activities are justified. He will start rumors that are false, steal information from desks and file drawers, and probe for administrative facts from Board of Education members who are naive about his goals, as well as unsuspecting personnel in the school system. He constantly keeps himself informed about all conflicts existing within the school system. Whenever possible he nurtures this conflict and develops political positions on non-important issues. The gang leader or the teacher education president is a shrewd, cunning, new breed, militant teacher. In most cases he is not interested in students nor subject matter. His only concern is with his own self gratification and the financial improvement of the situation. He is a union arts type, dedicated to the destruction of the system for the purpose of financial betterment. He is not an educator in any sense of the word and is not interested in the welfare nor benefit of children. He is self-centered, egotistical, and dedicated to a socialistic attitude toward public education. His interests are not in the best welfare of anyone but himself. His organization or gang is his shield to hide behind and his weapon to strike out with. The administration, board of education, and the rules and regulations which govern the school system are his enemies. Any discredit he can bring to his enemies contributes to the accomplishment of his goals. These gang leaders are leeches and parasites upon the public education process. Their followers are informers and warlords in the struggle to administer the schools. Their motives are nearly always doubtful and in very few instances can their methods be justified. They have sacrificed their educational ideals and prostituted their professional positions for the almighty dollar.

As you might imagine, membership in the gang is not compulsory but mandatory. This means that it is very difficult not to be a member. Subtle techniques are used by members to encourage new teachers to join. At the state and national level, teachers are contacted by teachers organizations during their second and third year of teacher training. Many of them join organizations while they are doing their teaching. These organizations brainwash them as to the good and the common goal of the association. Once these beginning teachers have been primed and lured into becoming members of the organization and they arrive on the local scene the local gang finishes the job. If they refuse to join, other teachers do not associate with them. If they continue to refuse, they are soon accused of being administrative patsies. They are left out

THE GANG

of teachers social events. And finally their performance in the classroom is discredited by the organization through rumor and lies which are spread in the community. Soon the teacher finds himself without a job. Thus, the gang has an unwritten rule that all new teachers must join or eventually be destroyed. If you are not a member of this new breed organization, then you are considered an enemy of it. It is a tightly organized highly structured independent political body. The leaders are cunning and masterful in the art of political intrigue. They thrive on using students and parents in a pressure attempt to influence boards of education by dividing them on issues and discrediting administrators within the public school structure. The majority of the members of these teacher gangs are followers. As followers, they do not consider the political issues just the political strategy. If one of their leaders decrees that some wrongdoing has injured one of their members, no questions are asked. The organization immediately mobilizes in defense of the teacher who has been allegedly mistreated. Before any information passes to the administration it must be filtered through the teacher organization leadership. Then if cleared, it may be passed along to an administrator through an appointed informer. The organization has appointed informers which are to develop relationships with various board members and administrators in order to feed certain factual information to them from the organization. By using this technique, the organization can provide the administration and board with certain information that will serve their purposes without being obligated to the credibility of the content. Administrative desk calendars are read on a regular basis by custodial personnel and loitering teachers and this information is passed back to the organization. Confidential documents concerning finances within the school system are sometimes stolen out of typewriters during lunch hours and copied for purposes of the organization. In remote cases offices are broken into during the night and file drawers ransacked in order to gain access to confidential facts. This information is then distorted and presented to the public in a manner which would be beneficial to the goals of the gang. The gang uses school paper and

THE GANG

copying machines to carry out their work as well as telephones and in some cases gasoline. The gang makes every attempt to utilize the resources of the normal school operation in pursuing their interest. If the gang leader happens to be a band leader, he may justify a telephone in his office as necessary to arrange concerts and band events. In other words every move that is made by the teacher organization to gain power within the school system is disguised as an educational essential of the system. Therefore, to the outsider the operation looks completely legitimate and normal. The membership thereby formulates their position within the system as legitimate. Every political and social maneuver becomes a means to an end in terms of the goals of the organization. The culminating and crowning satisfaction of the organization is to deliver an individual teacher to the position of continuing contract. The concept of continuing contract is simply lifetime guaranteed employment. In order to qualify for continuing contract it is necessary for a teacher to serve three consecutive years within the school district. Normally the teacher's performance is evaluated during those three consecutive years. Many school systems evaluate teachers twice a year usually around Christmas and then in May shortly before the school year is complete. During these evaluations it is common for an administrator within the district to actually visit the classroom for a short period of time. The administrator observes the teacher in the process of teaching and reviews the planning and system that the teacher is using to convey a subject matter. If the teacher seems to be well organized but has difficulty in certain areas which is common for beginning teachers, it is the administrator's responsibility to strengthen those areas through constructive criticism of the teaching method. If the teacher is successful in being evaluated twice a year for a three year period and continues to be employed by the school system, then the teacher is awarded at the recommendation of an administrator to the board, by the board a continuing contract. This simply means that the teacher cannot be dismissed from the school system for any less than gross neglect of duty, gross malfeasance of office, gross insubordination, or gross im-

THE GANG

morality. The latter has been defined by some to be proven immoral 144 times. In other words, it is almost impossible for school boards or an administrator to dismiss a teacher who has reached the all powerful position of continuing contract. Continuing contract is simply guaranteed lifetime employment by the school district disregarding special and extraordinary circumstances which rarely justify dismissal. Of course once a teacher reaches this privileged position within the system, that teacher can go about doing his duties in just about any way he chooses. For example, if he is weak in his planning or if he misses an unusual number of school days or decides to take a vacation in the middle of the school year even though he will be critized by the administration and could be reprimanded, it is highly unlikely that he will be dismissed even after repeated violations of regulations governing leave and social position. For this reason the members of the teachers organization during the apprentice period or three year test period of a beginning teacher will be encouraged to continue with the school system and of course advance in office in the teachers organization and their role in the teachers organization will be their payment for loyalty to the cause. In other words the gang takes care of its own. If a teacher is loyal to the gang and perpetuates the causes, supports the goals, and influences the internal political battles between the gang and the board of education during the three years of apprenticeship, that teacher is almost certain to be recommended for continuing contract and once that position is achieved the teacher will be gradually moved through the ranks of the teachers organization into a power position. Thus, loyalty is rewarded and the purpose and power of a strong gang is preserved.

Loyalty to the gang is all encompassing. A loyal gang member can be rewarded by being recommended to attend teachers conferences and represent the school district. A loyal gang member might become the object of praise of the local teachers organization. Or if a loyal gang member comes under close scrutiny and criticism from localites, that member could become the object or recipient of an award from a state teachers organization or another school district. In other words, it is impossible for a loyal gang member to come under the close scrutiny and observation and punitive discipline of an administrator or a school board. If this should happen by some strange quirk of fate that individual would be singled out by the local gang and supported in one of many ways. If direct support by making visible the strength of that individual was not adequate, then the gang would attempt to discredit the source of attack. If a principal or superintendent or supervisor within the school district seemed to be leveling criticism at the individual in question then the reproach of the gang would be to reciprocate criticism in the direction of the administrator. This could be carried out in many ways. A close review of the administrator's background might turn up a weakness in his preparation. For example, maybe he received a C in a course in college which was designed to help him observe teachers. Then the question might be asked if he was only an average student himself, when he was studying how to evaluate teachers, isn't it possible that he could be making a mistake. Possibly his private life has flaws. Maybe he is not a member of a local church. Or maybe he's not married and has been known to take social liberties upon occasion. It's even possible that the teachers organization could perpetuate a character assassination if the situation demands it. One way or the other the gang will survive and thrive within the organization and where necessary take advantage of any individual who might be critical of the gang as a whole or of an individual member. Loyalty rules supreme. The loyal gang member is safe and secure and will be protected at all costs and will survive the close scrutiny and criticism of any and all outsiders by developing an intense loyalty within each of the individual teachers. The organization is secure. Security is extremely important for many reasons. If the teachers can be counted on to be completely secure and loyal to the organization, the organization can protect its goals and secrets. If the teachers are completely loyal to the gang, the gang will not have to be concerned with information leaking to the opposition. When a struggle ensues between the gang and the board of education the gang can rest assured that there will be continuity, unity, and

THE GANG

loyalty from each member of the organization. Its plans will be secure and its political motives will be protected. Thus, security of the organization is all important to the membership. Security is reciprocal, if the organization is secure then the individual members are secure. Remember the gang is like a parent. It returns love and faithfulness and loyalty to the members. Remember as a beginning teacher one commonly would be insecure. Entering a new profession without experience, under the close scrutiny and watchful eye of experienced administrators, boards of education and parents, it is understandable that the young inexperienced teacher would feel insecure. However, under the protective wing of the teachers organization that insecure timid teacher becomes a haven of strength and courage. Knowing that if anything goes wrong the gang will be there to support him, the young insecure teacher goes about his duty under the security and blessing of the local organization. The teachers organization protects the beginning novice as well as encourages the new gang member to be loyal and preserve the right of the organization at any cost. As the new member is being indoctrinated, a planned method of supplying him with information concerning the value of the gang is perpetuated. Everyday one of the loyal old gang members approaches the novice and explains how the gang has helped over the years to protect her and provide for her. This impresses the young insecure teacher. Gradually the young teacher relies more and more upon the gang. As situations arise which threatens the security of the young gang member, the gang comes to the rescue with differing degrees of effectiveness. Over a period of time the young teacher depends and relies upon the protection and security of the membership. At this stage in the relationship between the gang and the new member, nothing is asked of the new member therefore, the gang seems like a friend of all and a wealth of security and strength. However, later the gang member will ask for the new teacher to pay the price. That price could be paid in the form of walking a picket line, of criticizing an administrator or of taking a stand on some critical social issue within the district. Sooner or later the young teacher will be

THE GANG

obligated to the organization and will pay the price the gang demands. To the furthest extreme that price could be the total support for a teacher within the system who is absolutely incompetent thus breaching the contract between what a teacher should do and what a teacher does. The moral obligation that every teacher accepts when they walk into a classroom is the responsibility to give of themselves so that students may learn. Once the teacher is willing to place personal security and monetary reward before the obligation to teach, the contract is broken and no obligation exists.

The teachers organization is a loyal secure protectorate of its membership, resistant to change and influence from without, absolutely right in the pursuit of its own goals and objectives, demanding and forceful in the enforcement of loyalty and security within the membership. The gang will survive regardless of the opposition. The small band of revolutionaries which control an individual school district have the backing of the total national organization which represents the gang at its strongest level. Therefore, if the resistance at the local level becomes too great, the gang will call for reinforcements from the state and national level. The concept of total unity is secure between the local, the state, and the national level. It is the responsibility of the local leaders to discipline the local membership and ensure that the local membership is loyal to the state and national leaders. Therefore, the local membership has protected the security of the gang and the reputation of the organization is protected and unity is preserved to resist the board of education and administration in the pursuit of worthy educational goals. The gang is right, the most important thing is power and money. In order to get more money for the organization it is necessary for the local gang to be demanding upon the board and the administration. Thus the pressure is on. Constantly the gang demands more money, less working hours, better working conditions, more equipment, less pupil contact time and on and on until the demands are so great and the pressures so overpowering that the board of education and administration crumble to defeat. If the demands alone are not enough to overpower the inexperienced board then the gang becomes forceful in the use of its popularity campaign against the students and the parents within the district. It is easy to justify a teacher's desire to be popular. But it is difficult to explain why a teacher would use popularity in order to influence a parent's vote. If the teacher can convince the students that he is indeed a friend then the students will in turn explain to the parents that the teachers are good and mean well. The parents in turn will vote for additional levies to provide salaries and fringe benefits for the teachers.

The professionalism has all but disappeared in education today. No longer is the professional educator concerned with idealism. The beginning teacher is taught by the teachers organization that the important thing is salary and fringe benefits. In other words education is teacher oriented not child oriented. No longer are educators concerned about how much a child learns or what values a child learns. The modern teacher is only concerned with how much salary is paid, how many days out of the school year must I actually be in the classroom and in fact how many minutes each day must I be exposed to children. There are obvious reasons why it is to the teachers organization and the individual teachers advantage to be concerned about these facts. For example, if there are ten teachers in a school and each teacher is only required to be exposed to students three hours a day, or four periods out of eight, then it takes twice as many teachers to accommodate the students during an entire school day. If it takes twice as many teachers it means that there are twice as many teaching jobs available which means the teachers organization can effectively place twice as many beginning teachers into job slots. This reasoning also means that the cost of education to the taxpayer doubles. In the old days ten teachers would teach approximately forty students per period for a total of eight periods in the day keeping in mind that they would have one period for lunch hour. Today that same situation has changed to the point that a teacher can negotiate through the teachers organization to teach a maximum of twenty-five students, a maximum of three periods a day and in turn has cut her or his exposure to a minimum and increased the need for more teachers and thus increased the number of teaching jobs available within the school district.

Thus the teacher has sacrificed idealistic professionalism for practical salary and fringe benefits. The teacher is now one of many no longer concerned about being a great teacher nor concerned about doing an above average job in the classroom. Once upon a time, teachers concerned themselves with the quality of instruction, with the thoroughness of preparation and with motivating students. Today teachers have set aside those idealistic goals in favor of conservative self-benefiting education.

What do teachers organizations think about money? Money is the grease of education. Money is used to grease the mechanisms that keep the machinery of education running. How does money work? First, high teaching salaries and high benefits increase the motivation of teachers. By motivating teachers, teachers are inclined to buy more equipment, supplies and textbooks which cost money. Remember that every mechanical teaching aid that is placed in the schools requires first less teacher time, less student exposure to teachers, and more tax money in terms of first the outright purchase of the equipment and second the maintenance of the equipment. This does not take into consideration the fact that the teachers must be trained to use the equipment and in turn students must be taught how to learn from a piece of equipment rather than from a teacher which detracts from the overall purpose of the school which is teaching subject matter. For example, let's assume that we place a teaching machine in the classroom in third grade reading, first the teacher must learn how to use the teaching machine, second the student must learn how to learn from the teaching machine, third the school board and in turn the taxpaying public must purchase the teaching machine, maintain it and in turn must pay for the teacher learning how to use it. What is the result of all this effort? In fact does the student learn more? In fact the student learns less, the teacher is required to teach less, the company that sells the teaching machine to the school ends up making a profit from the sale, the student eventually realizes that he is just one of many in the school and feels that he is not receiving enough individual attention from his teacher, thus it destroys his motivation to learn which in fact could be interpreted to mean that his parent's tax money was spent in order to destroy his individual motivation to learn. How can this be construed to be beneficial to the idealistic goals of education. Thus the teachers organization takes the position that money is paid by taxpayers to the schools for the benefit of teachers. In other words, taxpayers do not buy education, they buy direction on how to spend tax money from teachers who in turn are directed by teachers organizations. In fact one could conclude that teachers organizations spend taxpayers money in an inefficient manner in order to - 1. create more jobs for teachers, and 2. create more business for educational businesses that supply hardware in the form of textbooks and equipment to educational systems. When one stops to consider the logical conclusion one alternative must be that it is to the benefit of a teachers organization and in turn to the benefit of teachers to be inefficient in the educational process. In other words, if a teacher is ineffective in teaching students and in fact destroys the student's motivation to learn, then in turn it will cost the taxpaying public more money to educate that student and in turn will mean more dollars in the pockets of teachers and thus more loyalty from teachers to the teachers organization. Although this is a very logical conclusion to draw and is a realistic conclusion to develop after observing closely the actual influence of teachers and teachers organizations upon the system it is difficult to comprehend that an institutionalized system has been developed which would have these goals in mind.

One must consider that money and power and politics work together as a closely woven web designed to capture and consolidate the educational system. The teachers organization and the teachers work hand in hand in the effort to pull the web closely around the system in order to capture the tax money, the power that the tax money will buy, and to manipulate the politics which generate the tax money and keeps it flowing from the taxpayers to the tax spenders. The role of the teachers organization is primarily to manipulate educational politics in a manner that will facilitate the rapid flow of tax money from the taxpayers to the tax spenders. The tax spenders of course are the members of the teachers organizations or the individual teachers within the school district. Students suffer, parents suffer, the board of education suffers and the administration of the school suffer. The teachers organization wins, the gang develops loyalty within its membership and reinforces that loyalty with monetary gain in the form of salary and fringe benefits. The parents play the role of the bewildered taxpayer paying his taxes in order to keep the schools open for a purpose which he feels is beneficial to his children. The children watch the entire process. They watch their motivation being eroded by poor teaching techniques. They watch teachers waste money on equipment which does not do the job. They watch textbooks replaced by teaching aids which are ineffective. They watch their parents pay tax money and complain about it while in turn they don't realize that they're not getting their money's worth. They watch other students being passed through the organization without the benefit of learning. In other words students realize that they're not being educated but they have not reached a level of sophistication which allows them to share the results of their exposure to teachers, with their parents, in an understandable way. They complain about the schools, they complain about how they are treated but their complaints are passed off by their parents as normal complaints about the educational process. How can the parents, the board of education, and the administration all believe that teachers and teacher organizations are damaging the students they are entrusted with? To believe this means that one must develop an untrustful opinion of the entire educational system. To propose that the teachers organization is an institution which is undermining the very foundation of our society which is the strength of the values that we perpetuate through our educational process. The teachers organization then becomes an enemy of the public. It becomes a method of wasting both taxpayers money and children's time. It robs children of those years in the child's life when the child is most able and capable of learning. Thus it weakens a society by providing ill-prepared citizens to take roles of responsibility within the society. At the same time it perpetuates and reinforces both waste and inefficiency within the educational process. It does this by legitimizing poor education in the minds of children. These children then grow up to be parents and accept that when they were in school nothing educational took place. Therefore they are not surprised when their children learn nothing and since their parents paid taxes for very little education it seems quite logical that they should also pay taxes for even less education. Thus the circle is complete. The teachers organization completely controls the entire educational system and in turn controls the thinking of the parts of that system. It effectively controls the flow of tax dollars. It effectively controls the politics of the educational system, and by doing so it has the power to control the values within the society that are perpetuated by the educational system.

If we want the answer to why students at the college level seem less mature and less responsible than they did ten years ago, we should look to the process of which they are a product. If we look closely at what is being taught in the classroom we can understand why the product of that classroom thinks as it does. If we look closely at the procedures used to perpetuate the idealism of society and in turn to perpetuate the society we can understand why the society is in the condition that it is today. We can understand social disorder, we can understand crime, and a gradual erosion of the entire values of our system. Herein lies both the question and the answer within education. If the gang prevails. If the teachers organization continues. Eventually the total goal will be accomplished. All tax dollars will be spent for the purpose of perpetuating an educational institution which provides foremost for the teacher salaries and fringe benefits while at the same time provides in an inefficient manner the least possible education per grade level for each child. In effect this necessitates more teachers, creates more teaching jobs, while at the same time creates a demand for more teaching paraphernalia and does this at the expense of the individual student by robbing him or her of her naturally inherited right to be educated under the democratic system. The purpose of the gang is thereby completed. The gang has garnered the politics and the power and the money of the educational process. It perpetuates the use of the power, the politics, and the money at the expense of the students, the parents, the board, and the administration of the school district. It has captured the taxpayers in a web of inefficient use of resources and thus perpetuates the inflation of taxes upon the unsuspecting public. It creates a political climate in which the taxpaying public is defenseless against an erosion of values and social behavior within the society. As a result the society begins to crumble. The teachers organization has accomplished gang mentality. It has survived and prospered in a jungle of complicated finance and social behavior which it has designed and perpetuated.

CHAPTER IV

THE GANGSTERS

Some people might consider it a bit harsh to call the leaders of a teachers organization gangsters. However for the purpose of our interest, the term is very appropriate. We must consider that these leaders have an interest in robbing the children of our educational systems of their right to inherit the values and ethics of their ancestors. Of course they're not bank robbers nor do they drive around in big black limousines and carry shotguns. But they have certainly developed a system that rivals the great crime syndicates operating throughout the world. For the novice to educational organization it might be interesting to note that teachers throughout the United States are organized into local organizations which basically are the same as local unions or local crime syndicates. They also have a

THE GANGSTERS

state affiliate body which ties the teachers and their leaders in a local situation to the state leaders and the state organization. The state organization of course is tied to the National Association. At the national level the only thing at stake is power and politics. Children and education have long been forgotten, they exist only as a guise to legitimize a powerful systematic organization designed to reap taxpayer money and rob children of their deserved education. Thus the gangsters have their area leaders, their state leaders, and their national leaders. All hold an important power position in the total scheme of the organization. All of these leaders are proven loyal members of the order. Their behavior and decisions are completely supported by the total organization, thus an efficient swift moving system of calculating, intelligent, professional representatives has been turned into a corrupt, politically oriented, wealth seeking organization of radical reformers within the existing educational system. A sub-structure has been implanted below the existing organizational structure of the total U.S. educational system and that sub-structure has replaced normal ethical goals which we attach to our present system and in turn has replaced those goals with self-serving political goals of the organization which we call the gang.

As with any organization the gangsters have good and bad followers. The good followers of course are the loyal conscientious proven members of the gang. The bad followers are those teachers who still maintain a similance of idealism toward education. In other words, if a teacher conscientiously tries to develop a strong educational program within her classroom and concentrates more on the education of children than on the political welfare of the gang, then that teacher is a bad gang member. The ideal gang member frees himself from all educational duties within the school system. For example, he might take an advisory role to several groups within the school such as the school newspaper or the golf team or possibly some other organization within the school. Once he has been assigned to duties which do not tie him to the classroom and which free his time for political involvement, then he ties this free time into the teachers organization and becomes a strong deeply imbedded gang

THE GANGSTERS

member. The teacher might have ulterior motives for becoming a loyal gang member. For example, the teacher might have been recently evaluated and criticized by the school administration The teacher's performance in the classroom might not be acceptable. The teacher might be a homosexual. The teacher might have been involved in some way taking advantage of students under his direct control. All of these situations could have developed in such a way that the teacher received criticism from the administration, the board, or the community at large. In this situation a teacher coming under criticism with a strong possibility of more criticism because he lacks the capacity to provide the kind of education that we expect, finds refuge and protection by becoming a member of the gang, becoming closely tied to the teachers organization, and performing functions within the organization which could be termed dirty tricks.

What type of "dirty tricks" do these teachers participate in. It's possible that they could play the role of a spy or informer within the school district. In this role they might develop close allegiance and friendship with school principals and other administrators in order to find information concerning the internal politics of the system. These information gatherers then report the information back to the central leaders of the gang. The gang leaders synthesize the information from several of the informers and develop that information into a political strategy for the purpose of obtaining higher salaries and greater fringe benefits within the system. Other dirty tricks could involve spreading malicious rumors concerning the school district. For example, if a board should happen to criticize a teacher, take our homosexual English teacher for example. This teacher threatened students with poor or failing grades in order to develop a student depending upon himself. He would then after failing a student he had targeted for his affections several times invite that student to his home for remedial training. The unsuspecting student would arrive at his apartment thinking that he was going to get a special English lesson from his teacher. In fact as the evening developed the teacher would make sexual advances toward the young boy. This would

THE GANGSTERS

culminate in the boy telling his parents about the situation. Of course, all the time he would be threatening the boy with failure in the classroom should he divulge the activities. Gradually the situation would become known in the district although on a superficial familiarity. A board member suddenly makes a comment at a board meeting concerning the behavior of that particular teacher. It might develop that the board member does not even publically state that there is a problem. Maybe the parent talked with the board member and included him in on the comments made by the student in question. The board member casually mentions the situation to the superintendent who in turn discusses it briefly with the principal of the school. The informer who has implanted himself close to the principal to pick up any negative vibrations concerning any of the loyal gang members picks up the rumor that one of the teachers in the school is suspected of having homosexual relations with one or more students. The informer rushes to the gang leader with this morsel of savory information. The gang leader synthesizes the information and places it in context.

THE GANGSTERS

The gang leader being wise and knowledgeable and well informed concerning all the activities of his gang immediately recognizes the situation as dangerous. He realizes if one of his gang members is dismissed on charges of homosexuality that this could damage the reputation of the gang in the local area. At the same time he realizes that the homosexual gang member has been very loyal to the gang in many difficult situations. He remembers this particular homosexual gang member walking the picket line during the last organization strike. He remembers that this particular gang member has helped siphon board funds and involved him in several educational workshops that he would not otherwise have been involved in. He realizes that this gang member has printed posters and distributed them within the community which were anti-administration and board. Thus, the gang leader decides that a strategy must be developed to save the homosexual's reputation and preserve continuity within the gang. The gang leader then meets with his executive committee and they develop a political strategy which sabotages the reputation of

THE GANGSTERS

the board member who originally questioned the moral integrity of the teacher involved. The strategy involves a character assassination of the board member within the community. The informers within the teachers oranization are told to gather any negative type of information concerning the board member who made the accusations about the homosexual teacher. The informers gather bits and pieces of information concerning the sexual life, the financial life and personal behavior of the board member in question. Perhaps the board member occasionally drinks alcohol or is in debt or is not particularly religious or is involved in a personal affair within the community. All of these facts and many more will be developed by the informers and reported back to the gang leaders. The gang leaders will then correlate, filter, and editoralize the information that the gang informers provide about the personal behavior of the board member. All of this information will then be developed into a carefully organized political plan which will ultimately destroy the character of the board member who attacked a gang member. The information will be then sent out through loyal gang members and they will in turn spread the malicious rumors among the students within the school district, the students will then carry the information home to their parents who eventually will demand that the board member be removed from the board for one of many personal character offenses which developed as a result of the gang activity. Thus the circle is complete. A board member attacks a teacher. The teacher counter attacks through the teachers organization and destroys the board member. The board member is faced with a character assassination developed by the teachers' gang. Eventually the board member is defeated in the election by teacher votes and votes of those taxpayers who have heard the malicious rumors spread by the teachers organization. At the same time the homosexual teacher feels stronger and more confident in his position within the district. He continues and accelerates his homosexual harassment of students and feels confident that he is solidly protected from any retaliation from the school administration or board. The school administration withdraws from the situation

THE GANGSTERS

seeing the devastating effect the character assassination had upon the board member who criticized the organization. Thus the scenario is played once and twice again until all of the enemies of the local gang have been destroyed. The political manipulation of the gang members is total and complete. It handles all threatening situations at the expense of the students.

Being in this favored position within the school system the gang members are knowledgeable about the internal workings of the system and they have time to get involved in the political manipulation of the organization. Since the gang members are the teachers they are respected in the community due to the age old respect that we traditionally ascribe to educators. They hold positions within the system which free them from pupil contact. In fact the goals of the teachers gang are to be exposed to students as little as possible, in other words, if I am a teacher I can be exposed to students two 45-minute periods a day and be assigned to supervisory and planning activities the other six hours during the day, then in fact I have six hours to be involved in political operations within the organization. I have six hours to collect information to meet with the executive committee to develop political strategies which will improve the strength of the gang within the system. I have people working within the organization as informers who will bring information to me which I can build into political strategies. I have the time, knowledge, and a favored position within the school system which I can apply to the goals of the gang. As an individual I would be weak, I would only have one vote, I could only achieve my individual goals by becoming a strong gang member and thus directing the loyalty of the gang toward my individual goals in terms of gaining greater salary, fringe benefits, and freedom within the educational structure. Eventually I will be able to dictate the evaluation procedure which will be used to evaluate my performance within the classroom. Eventually I will be able to laugh in the face of an administrator when he accuses me of homosexually abusing students within the school district. Knowing that first he cannot prove his accusations and second that he cannot dismiss me from the district because of the tremendous retaliation potential

THE GANGSTERS

that I have as a strong member of the teacher gang. I will be able to eventually destroy that administrator and have him dismissed from the system through repeated character assassination over a period of time with the help of gang members collecting, synthesizing, and developing political character assassinations toward the administrator in question.

In general, it could be said that teachers' organizations place politics first and education second on their priority list. This means that time, effort, and money is expended by the gang for the development of a strong organization within the school system. This political substructure strives to gain control of the total resources of the system at the expense of the students involved. All ethics are abandoned in the pursuit of control over the resources of the system. Schemes and plots are devised to take advantage of the system, resources and utilize the funds which have been allocated by taxpayers for education instead, for the benefit of teachers. The gang reaps the benefits of political manipulation within the system. The gang members are rewarded for contributions to the gang effort, the entire process is an undermining of the traditional values of education. The gang establishes a sub-structure which replaces an educational system devoted to student improvement with an educational system devoted to teacher welfare. The entire educational system becomes a teacher welfare program. Efforts of the board and administration are expended on satisfying teacher needs and not on satisfying student needs. Thus the gang develops both total control and total authority over all of the resources within the system and takes advantage of this new power position in every conceivable way at the expense of both the students and parents who pay for the system.

The gang is a power hungry organization with dictatorial control on the national level and is operated in a dictatorial manner at all levels. Authority is delegated from the national to the state to the local and the battles for political power rage in all sectors. The ultimate goal of the gang is to endorse political candidates in national elections to Congress, Senate, and Presidency. As their candidates are endorsed they control the

THE GANGSTERS

vote of the membership of their organization and in turn lobby for educational benefits in the form of increased taxes to finance the national educational system. Once their campaign to elect leaders and raise taxes in an effort to pour more funds into the system, they in turn use political subversion to undermine the basic purpose of the system and regain the use of those funds for individual needs and benefits. Through this complexed "carrot and stick" technique the teachers organizations have been able to influence the public into paying more taxes for less education than ever before in the history of the country. In fact they have been able to elect leaders to establish a broader tax base for support of educational programs while at the same time using those funds ineffectively and insufficiently and for the individual benefit of the teachers involved thus disregarding the purpose of education in our society which is to perpetuate a value system to the youth of America.

Most gang members are dissatisfied and displeased with the salary and fringe benefits of the system. However, the system is usually also dissatisfied with them. Let's look at the typical profile of a gang member. For our purpose let's consider Independent Irene, a second grade teacher. She is married and her husband provides well for her. Thus, her salary is the second wage for the family. This gives her independence and a special financial position within the system. Independent Irene is difficult to control since she does not need her job to survive, she has little interest on satisfying the administration of the school. She then develops habits such as coming to work late, since it is not required that she punch a time clock, leaving early and refusing to take extra work assignments since she always has a ready excuse that her family needs her after school. In order to maintain this rather responsibility-free position within the system, she becomes a loyal gang member and after three years in the system she gains tenure which means that she can only be dismissed for malfeasance, insubordination, or gross immorality. In this position she becomes a self appointed critic of the school system. She does the least possible amount of preparation for her classes. Since she has three years of teaching experience and she is teaching the second grade, it is not difficult for her

THE GANGSTERS

to bluff her way through day after day with time consuming repetitious busy work for her students. The result of course is that the students receive little or no second grade education. This does not show up in terms of student performance for at least three of four years when national test norms are applied to student achievement. However, the students still do not learn. She feels secure that over the next eight years of their public education, they will make up what she has not taught them. So therefore she rationalizes that the loss of the second grade is not a great traumatic experience. Her students like her because she has little games for them to play, and songs for them to sing, movies for them to watch, and celebrates all of the holidays with a party in the classroom. Therefore, the students go home and tell the parents that Independent Irene is a great second grade teacher. The parents come to the PTA meeting and they find that Independent Irene was sick on the night of the meeting and couldn't make it, so they go home with no impression at all. Another example of a typical gang member is Religious Raymond. Religious Raymond is a bachelor. He is a very religious individual. He attends all the church meetings in the community and is in choir on Sunday, he looks religious in his manner. Oh, he is very well dressed with a necktie and a clean shirt, his hair closely cut, and always the first to criticize any act which could be construed immoral or even a little on the unacceptable side. Religious Raymond has even been known to start the day with a prayer in his classroom. Occasionally he sees fit to read sections of the Bible to his students since he is an eighth grade social studies teacher it is easy for him to work the historical value of various religious sects into his natural subject matter. He uses his image as a teacher in the community to hide his religious fanaticism. However, in his classroom the fanaticism surfaces and he conveys along with the subject matter a strong religious bias to his students. Thus, the students receive during their eighth grade social studies class ten to twenty percent subject matter and seventy to eighty percent religious thoughts and interpretations filtered through Raymond's viewpoint. Of course, Religious Raymond is evaluated according to the system's evaluation schedule and he has been cited

THE GANGSTERS

a couple of times by his principal for involving too much religion in his history class. Raymond, of course, takes a very pioused view toward these criticisms and feels the administration is more or less against religion. He feels he is doing God's work by carrying the word to his eighth grade students, he feels he is being picked upon by the administration and he hides his lack of subject matter knowledge about history behind his fanaticism for religion. In order to protect himself of course he has gained a position as a tenured gang member. He is loyal to the gang because the gang protects him from the criticism of the administration and the community about his religious involvement and whenever he is criticized he relies on the gang to once again save him from those individuals within the system who are against his Godly nature. Down the hall from Religious Raymond we have Incompetent Henry, a ninth grade math teacher. Henry became a teacher because he couldn't find anything else he could do. The phrase "those who can, do and those who can't, teach" applies to Henry. Henry can't do anything. He has no manual skills and he lacks a quick mind or the knowledge or desire to participate in any phase of life. His only asset is that his parents sent him to college and he learned enough math to teach ninth grade arithmetic. Thus, Incompetent Henry hides in the ninth grade math class teaching the same textbook year after year for the last ten years. He's very secure in his position, he never changes his technique, he has mapped out every single day of the year in the form of a lesson plan. He knows exactly what he's going to do every day and he does the same thing day after day after day. He never attends any training sessions to upgrade teachers, he resists all new teaching techniques, all new teaching methods and all new textbooks and teaching materials. He clings to the old math textbook that he used his first year of teaching. And even though the publisher no longer publishes that book because it is obsolete, Incompetent Henry demands that they reprint copies and he's very careful to tell his students not to damage the books. In some of his classes the books have been rebound two and three times and he will not change textbooks even though funds are available and many parents and students have asked why do we use these old textbooks in ninth grade math when there are so many new modern books on the market. The answer of course is that Incompetent Henry is afraid to change to a new text because his lesson plans won't fit it and it may be difficult for him to learn. Also, there's always a chance that the students will learn it faster than he does and it would be very embarrassing for him to teach. Thus, Incompetent Henry looks to the gang for protection whenever anybody threatens his world with a new innovation in math, he immediately hides behind the power of the organization to protect him. On the second floor of our typical school we find Ronnie Rummy, the school alcoholic. Ronnie is close to retirement age, he only has three more years before he's turned out to pasture. Ronnie has always had a little drinking problem but the last five years it has developed into a social problem. Ronnie has a few drinks before he comes to school in the morning and of course once in awhile the principal or one of the students will notice a trace of alcohol on his breath. Ronnie's sole ambition in life is to complete three more years as a tenured teacher and face into retirement. He does as little as possible in his English class. We know that students do not readily appreciate English in the seventh grade anyway. Ronnie Rummy teaches English in any way the students like it. He calls it contract teaching. The student develops a set of experiences that they want to involve themselves in and then they talk with Ronnie about it and they agree on a timetable as long as the student completes all of the experiences that he has built into his contract, Ronnie agrees and passes the student on to the next grade level. Ronnie always eats lunch away from the school grounds and lately has been late coming back sometimes missing the period shortly after lunch. Ronnie misses several days a year due to ill health. Although he has never been able to find a physician who would attest to any illness. Ronnie has social and psychological problems. Thus, he looks to the teachers organization to protect him, it's important that he maintain his position as an English teacher for three more years so that he can complete his tenure and drift into retirement where he will no longer be bothered each day by a classroom, a schedule, or students and he will

THE GANGSTERS

have all of his time to do that which he does best and enjoy life and alcohol. Further down the hall we come upon our special education class. These students all have an IQ under 50 or mental age of about eight years old. Of course their physical age is fourteen to sixteen. Since the IQ's of the students are so low, Sexy Sam, their fifth year teacher, only has five students to teach. Sexy Sam is a young playboy type individual. Sexy Sam has been known to come to school with his shirt unbuttoned, wearing sandals, and he's always reading the latest Playboy magazine. Sexy Sam has little Susie Sexpot in his class. Susie Sexpot has a mental age of eight and a physical age of sixteen. She becomes the object of Sexy Sam's attention day in and day out throughout the school year. Sexy Sam being a dedicated teacher of course has arranged for Susie Sexpot to accompany him on several outings on the weekend. Some of these outings involve camping trips and sight-seeing tours of a local zoo. Of course Sexy Sam gets along very well with the parents of all of his students since he shows a tremendous interest in the students. His interest is carried far beyond the daily classroom work. Sometimes Sexy Sam turns out the lights in the classroom and they play games. Since Sexy Sam only has five students and the highest mental age is eight, the games are a lot of fun. Thus to all onlookers Sexy Sam is a dedicated young teacher interested in the welfare of his students. However, Sexy Sam again looks to the teachers organization to protect his position within the school. If he is criticized by one of his students for being too friendly, Sexy Sam wants to know that the organization will support him. He wants to know that if an irate father approaches him asking him why it's necessary to turn the lights off in the classroom, that he will have an organization and friends behind him to support his unusual teaching techniques. If an irate mother asks why the Playboy magazine appeared in Sexy Sam's special ed class, Sexy Sam wants assurance that other teachers will attest to his credibility.

Thus, all of our teaching staff has one factor in common — insecurity and instability and a need for dependence upon a gang. All of these individuals are in one way or another misfits within the society, yet they bring their strong bias

THE GANGSTERS

and individual maladjustment to the classroom and pass it on to the students that they teach. They not only teach subject matter but they teach their own unusual personality maladjustments. In fact the greatest impression this group has upon the students is its own personality. That personality cannot be changed nor can it be influenced by the evaluation system of the administration nor the board of education. The reason it cannot be changed or altered is because the gang is too strong, the gang is too well organized, it has the power to protect the individual members from any constructive criticism of the educational system. Thus the administrators in the school are dissatisfied with the teaching performance, they are very much aware of the individual personality misfits of the teachers, while at the same time they are cognizant of the fact that they cannot take constructive action toward changing the methods and personalities of those teachers who are entrusted with the development of the students under their control. The staff in turn develops a gang mentality for its own protection and interest in money and not education, an interest in freedom within the classroom without outside control and a militant radical calculation attitude toward any individual or group within the system who threatens their longevity. Thus, they become an organized, brainwashed, dishuman gang of personality misfits who are hiding behind the traditional image of teacher.

The students, the parents, the board of education, the school system, and the values of our society suffer as a result of placing incompetent personality misfits in charge of our youth. Susie Sexpot and Sexy Sam would make an excellent couple to attend the annual convention of regional lunatics. However, we expect more than to find them carrying out their social disorders at the expense of the taxpaying public. Independent Irene would be great as a farmer's helper but we expect more from a dedicated teacher. Ronnie Rummy would be the life of the party at a Playboy convention but in his eighth grade history class he is a trifle misplaced. In essence we expect those people who are obliged and employed to perpetuate the values which we consider to represent twelve years of public education and who

THE GANGSTERS

are entrusted with the formation of value systems within the minds of our youth to carry a reasonable image in terms of self behavior. However, when their behavior is more radical and more deviate than what is traditionally accepted, we would expect that there is a way that the system can release these individuals or at least help them reconstruct their own values.

In the beginning the system had a means to repair itself. Evaluation systems and screening procedures were applied by the administration and as a result constructive criticism led to beneficial changes of behavior within the staff and the organization, thus the system was kept intact and strong. The gang and the gang mentality has changed all of that. Instead of accepting constructive criticism the gang actively supports and defends what would have at one time been unacceptable social behavior within the classroom. The gang is such a formidable opponent to traditional values that the board and administration no longer has an even chance of redeeming maladjusted behavior. Our system not only condones poor teaching and unacceptable social behavior within the ranks of its staff, but it also finances the perpetuation of the value systems of its staff and reinforces distorted behavior patterns among the gang members. Thus, the gang has both the method for perpetuating its own existence and the means for financing the policies that it protects.

Independent Irene, Religious Raymond, Incompetent Henry, Ronnie Rummy, and Sexy Sam become the pillars of our society supported with our tax dollars and our lack of interest in what really goes on behind the closed classroom door. They are protected by the gang which they created, thus they become the children robbers. In terms of the society they have an above average education, they are knowledgeable, they have a favored position within the school system and a position of authority from which they can perpetuate their hunger for power and their dissatisfaction with life. As students are robbed of their right to an education and parents are robbed of their tax dollars and the school system is robbed of teaching performance which it has paid for, the gang enjoys the privileged environment which it has created. It enjoys the fringe benefits and the salaries it has pressured the system into providing. The children robbers feast upon their own ineffectiveness. They celebrate upon the corpse of the system which they have sacrificed. Thus, the gangsters survive as the system crumbles. The children robbers reign supreme while the students and the taxpayers cry for mercy and justice. The circle of power is now complete. Once in the hands of those who formed it, the power has shifted to those who would abuse it. The system is now owned by those who were supposed to serve it. No longer can the children robbers be relied upon to pass on their knowledge and the traditional values of the system. All that remains is total abuse of the system upon abuse of the finances upon abuse of the people for which the system was formed to serve. Once this system has been devoured, the robbers nurtured by their own aggression will attack the society as a whole, critical of its values, self indulging of its resources.

CHAPTER V

THE HIDEOUT

Every gang has a hideout and the teachers organization is no exception. What is a hideout? A hideout is a place where the gang members plan their strategy. It's a place for them to rest and relax and share their victories with each other. It is a home for the gang. It is a well-equipped, functional location, convenient to gang members and convenient to communication channels. It's a place where telephone accessibility is readily available. It's a place where you feel protected and where you are familiar with the environment and surroundings. For the teachers gang, the hideout is the school. The total school not just the individual teacher's classroom. In fact, the entire school has been taken over by the gang and all of the facilities, equipment and even the secretarial help which has been

THE HIDEOUT

assigned to individual gang members, is now used for the purpose of subverting the original purpose of the institution.

The classroom, for example, is now a storage place for documents and strategies developed by the teachers organization. It is also used for committee meetings of the teachers organization. Stop a minute and think what other organization supplies telephone service, secretarial service, a warm or air conditioned meeting area anytime of the day or night plus the added conveniences of an auditorium for large group meetings, or a bus system which can be used to transport teachers to local or state level meetings. All these facilities are provided at no cost to the union which is in opposition to the management of the schools. What other union has it so well? What other union can use the resources of the institution to combat its control? If the teachers organization needs something duplicated, there are plenty of duplicators within the school, the paper is free, the labor supplied by some student and in fact the literature is duplicated at no cost to the organization and circulated at no cost to the organization by sending it home with students. If telephone calls are necessary, there are always key members of the organization who have telephones in their private offices. Some of these individuals might include the band director who has, of course, a legitimate use for a telephone since he must schedule the band at each athletic activity, or the head athletic director who also has a legitimate need for a telephone. A distributive education teacher possibly needs a telephone to set up interviews for perspective job applicants. However, these phones are not in the main office of the school, but they can be used for teacher organization business and in many cases are. In fact, every type of supply that is used in the regular classroom for legitimate purposes is also used by the teachers organization for illegitimate purposes. Through this mesmerizing technique of converting that which is illegitimate to legitimate by intermingling legitimate business with illegitimate activity, the teachers organization has cleverly developed a situation where they have the total resources of the school at their convenience. In other words, the school is a well-equipped functional hideout for a subversive group of

THE HIDEOUT

radical union members. The teachers lounge is just one such location. It provides a centralized convenient location to display teacher organization literature thus keeping all of the gang members well informed. It supplies a recreational facility to develop comradery between gang members. The extra-curricular program of the school justifies gang members being in the school at all hours of the day and night. Since it is costly for the board of education to supervise teachers during the extra-curricular hours, it is possible for a coach or a band director to be in the school on a Saturday morning, afternoon, evening or anytime without supervision. Thus, it is possible for him to use this time to develop strategies, work on projects, use school facilities, make long distance telephone calls, and in general turn the entire institution into a subversive center of activity. Who is responsible for policing the use of the school as a hideout? First, it is impossible for the administration to keep track of the individual activities of all the teachers in the school. This is especially true if certain teachers are doing everything under their control to utilize the resources available to them for subversive activities. For example, if an administrator decides he is going to make the auditorium off limits for teachers during non-school hours, immediately a teacher raises a legitimate need for the auditorium. He indicates that he must set up his visual equipment for his next class which he's teaching in the auditorium during regular school hours. The principal then looks ridiculous. He's denying a teacher the use of a school facility for a legitimate purpose. Thus, the principal backs down on his original position and opens up the auditorium. However, instead of using the auditorium for legitimate purposes, the teacher invites three or four gang members and holds an unofficial committee meeting in the auditorium. Of course, slide projectors and other audio visual aids are present, but the purpose of the meeting is not to prepare for the following day's class, but to prepare for political maneuvers within the teachers organization. Thus, it is impossible to separate the legitimate from the illegitimate within the confines of the institution. The administrator is left at best with a cursory, superficial, supervisory control over the hideout. Organization meetings are held at the school without restriction.

The community is completely unaware that the school has been taken over internally by the teacher gang. The community realizes that Al Smith, football coach, is always working on weekends. They see his automobile at the school and they think nothing of it. What they don't know is that his time is being spent developing a strategy for negotiating with the board of education for more salary and fringe benefits. That strategy could even include reduced exposure to students. Since his primary purpose for being employed by the school is to be exposed to students and to teach them something, it is absolutely contrary to his purpose to be using the facility of his employer to develop a strategy against teaching. The community is unaware that the central office of the school is infiltrated. Basically there are two organizations within the school. One is the teachers organization and one is an organization for non-teaching employees. Although there's a very close relationship between these two organizations, not until recently have they developed a strong unity of purpose. The secretary to the superintendent, of course, is a member of the non-teaching organization. However, since the purpose of both organizations is basically to improve salaries and fringe benefits, all information which is processed by the administrative offices is more or less available to the teachers organization. Unless you have an unusual situation where one or two individuals have developed strong loyalty for the people for whom they work, it is completely possible that the superintendent's secretary might also hold an office in the non-teaching organization and thus be more than willing to share all information which moves through that office with the teacher gang. The credibility gap thus widens and includes all teachers and non-teacher employees within the school system with the exception of a few administrators and the board of education. These two groups are also gradually being infiltrated and included with the purposes of the organization. If a new board member is elected who is sympathetic to the teachers organization, the new board member is gradually compromised into a position where he is working with the

THE HIDEOUT 149

organization against the purpose of the system which is to provide an efficient effective education for children. Administrators realizing that their only path to survival is cooperation, also gradually develop strong unity and loyalty for the organization. In fact, in some schools all administrators, teachers, and board members are 100 percent behind the purposes of the teachers organization which is 100 percent against the goals of the community and the taxpayers who pay the bill.

Let's look closer at how the hideout serves the gang. In one situation the teachers gang needed a few hundred dollars in order to finance a heated political campaign within the community against the board of education. Their scheme involved the use of the shop facility within the school. The shop teacher who was a talented refrigerator repairman isolated one section of the shop and placed a padlock on it. He then put an ad in a local newspaper for a refrigerator repair service listing his home telephone number. People would call wanting their refrigerators and air conditioners and other appliances repaired. He would in turn take them to his home. Since he was a teacher in the community he was well known and respected and business was good. What the community was unaware of was that he in turn would take the appliances to the school and teach his students how to repair them. He would order parts for the refrigerators and other appliances through his school budget, the parts would be sent into the school, the refrigerators and appliances would be repaired, he would take them back to his home on the weekend and they in turn would be picked up by the owner and the bills paid. Occasionally he would use the school van to haul the appliances to and from his home. He would even send students on errands using the school van to purchase parts and materials needed to repair the appliances. All of the funds were then channeled back through the teachers organization. Not only was this an illegitimate business being operated within the school at taxpayers expense, but it was also illegal since no taxes were paid on the income and the income was being diverted into the organization in order to finance a subversive political activity of the organization aimed at under-

THE HIDEOUT

mining the school and the board of education. The result of this activity was that the teachers received a sizeable increase in salary during the next negotiation session with the board. The same type of operation was developed within another school in the automotive shop where the teacher would advertise in the community for old junk automobiles which he could use for instructional purposes. The junk automobiles would be brought into the shop, parts would be purchased to repair them through the school budget, and student labor would be used to put them into good condition. Once the entire project was complete, the automobile would be sold, although the teacher would claim that it had been junked. The result would be income for the individual teacher and the teachers organization at taxpayers expense and tax free. The same type of activity is carried on in the home economics classes where students work all week on various projects making bread and cookies to be sold at a bake sale at the end of the week. All the food was purchased through the board of education budget. Sometimes by checking the home economics budget you can see that four or five hundred dollars worth of food per week is used. Where does the food go? In many cases it is sold on the weekend at a bake sale to raise money to finance an activity of the teachers organization. Some of those activities include trips to national conventions and other travel activities financed internally within the organization. No accountability is required for the funds of these organizations within the school. Since the teachers organization is very closely related with the non-teaching employees organization, the cafeteria comes into focus. The next time you hear students complaining because the cafeteria food is poor in the school, look closely at the situation and you might find that the funds are being diverted. How does this happen? In one case the state provided several hundred pounds of hamburger, several hundred cases of tomato sauce, and several hundred pounds of white enriched flour so that the school could provide pizza to the students at a reduced cost. Since the students were complaining about the quality of the pizza being served, the administration discovered that there was a local Italian restaurant in the community that was purchasing all

THE HIDEOUT

of its supplies from the manager of the school cafeteria. As you can see, this could be a very profitable operation since all the supplies purchased were donated through the State Department to the school and in turn sold by the manager of the cafeteria to a local restaurant at a reduced cost. The situation became so obvious that at one point, the manager of the restaurant ran short on flour during a rush period and called the administrator of the school, not knowing that he was not in on the plan, and asked him to deliver a couple hundred pounds of flour to his restaurant. Shortly afterward the situation was discovered and put to an end. Another situation developed when a local businessman asked the band director to bring the band to the airport to greet the president of his company. Of course, this made a nice extra-curricular activity for the band members and the band rode to the airport on a school bus paid for at taxpayers expense and in turn the businessman made a nice donation of five hundred dollars to the band. The businessman felt that this was a legitimate use of public funds. The band director felt it was a wonderful fund raising technique and did not account for the five hundred dollars, but in turn used the funds to finance a teacher organization project. The hideout thus provides facilities ranging from musical instruments to cafeteria supplies to buses, automobiles, and trucks to expense accounts, which can all be used for the purpose of the organization against the administration of the school. If these resources are cleverly manipulated, it is impossible to differentiate between the legitimate use of facilities, equipment, and funds for the educational purposes of the institution, and the illegitimate use of facilities, equipment, and funds for the illegitimate purposes of the gang.

In one case a one half million dollar closed circuit television station was developed within a school for instructional purposes. Programs were to be developed on English, Math, Social Studies, and closed circuit cameras and television monitors were purchased for use within the classroom. Within a short time a school levy was up for election. All of this equipment was used to develop TV editorials supporting the teachers organization and the levy attempt. Of

THE HIDEOUT

course, the levy was successful within the community since the quality of advertising was so professional. The result of the levy renewal increased the teachers salaries within the community and the fringe benefits of the employees. However, it had no direct positive effect upon the instruction within the school.

Simply stated, the hideout is an unlimited warehouse of resources used by the teachers organization to develop and perpetuate the clandestine purposes of the gang, and at the same time destroy the supervision and control of the organization by the administration and board of education of the school. Every single resource from a paper clip to a television station within the school is used for the purpose of the organization to perpetuate control over the system and justify and legitimize the lack of education within the system.

Thus, the better equipped more modern the hideout, the stronger and more efficient the gang. If the hideout within your community is a ultra-modern, well-equipped facility, then you may be assured that the gang is strong. And remember, the stronger the gang within the community, the less likely you are to know the activities of the group. The more likely you are to have a favorable opinion of their functions and activities due to the public relations campaign that they have developed and released upon the community through the use of the facilities and equipment provided by the community. All in all, without the hideout, the gang is left without facilities to operate. They become an organization without resources. This situation is taken care of by shared resources. For example, if there is a weak gang with a poorly-equipped hideout near a strong gang with a well-equipped hideout, the well-equipped hideout is shared until the weak gang develops their own resources and base of operation. This piggy back effect strengthens the overall unity of the state-wide organization while pulling the membership in the close unity through common purpose. Thus, your well-equipped, ultra modern facility, paid for with local tax dollars, could be supporting a nearby teachers gang in a poor district who is using your tax money to help promote the political purpose of a neighboring institution.

THE HIDEOUT

It is not unusual for an expensive stereo system to be purchased by the music department of a high school and find itself resting in the home of a board member who supported the salary increase for the local teachers organization. In one instance, an entire home was purchased for special education program. The home was reoutfitted, repainted, and put in tip top repair during the first year it was owned by the board of education. Two years later, the home was sold at a loss to a board member who moved into a well-furnished, completely well-maintained facility as his reward for support of the local teachers organization.

Remember, the next time you look at a school, it is a school to you, but for somebody it is a hideout. The hideout provides everything from recreational facilities for gang social activities to business facilities for gang money raising activities. More and more board members are included in the social activities of the gang and rewarded through taxpayer dollars. Familiarity with teachers is commonplace and the misuse of public funds is legitimized. The hideout is an all important tool in the quest for gang power. It provides an unlimited resource of centralized facilities and a base of operation all in one location. Who would suspect the local school of being a hideout for a radical, subversive, political organization aimed at the destruction of education. Thus, the secret goes on, gang members come and go, but the hideout only improves in its efficiency and effectiveness as the organization redirects taxpayers funds toward its own purposes.

CHAPTER VI

THE PRIZE

In every contest there must be a prize. The situation is not any different between the teachers organization or the gang and the public school system of the U.S. However, in all contests there are usually prizes for different levels of achievement. In the contest between the gang and the U.S. educational system there are also prizes at all levels. The ultimate prize on a grand scale, of course, can be defined as complete control over all funds from the national budget to the state budget to the local school district. This can be accomplished through uniting the entire teacher movement throughout the United States in an effort to endorse political candidates for the Presidency, the Congress, and the Senate who are sympathetic to the demands of education. This can be accomplished through the manipulation and utilization of money, equipment, and facilities which have been designated for the purpose of educating America's youth. However, by channeling and directing this enormous wealth of power toward the purpose of lobbying and subverting the intention of the system, the prize ultimately can be accomplished.

However, it is commonplace for team members to receive individual prizes for recognition of their efforts toward the total team purpose above and beyond the call of duty. So we must first examine the prize for winning the total contest which in essence is the struggle for control of the total educational system of the country. Then we must look at the secondary prizes which become the awards for the team participants on the winning side.

The greatest reward an actual teacher can receive as a result of the struggle is a guaranteed salary and fringe benefit program which is above average in terms of total income of the working population of the U.S. and a guaranteed retirement program which includes health and medical benefits for the remainder of their life and/or their spouses lives. How would you like to have a job which requires you to work 180 days a year which guaranteed you all national holidays, all weekends free, which guaranteed you a certain amount of time out of every day to be spent according to your own personal fancy? The job also guarantees you health and medical fringe benefits after retirement and eventually would give you full retirement pay at the level of your five highest salary years during your employment. It also provides you with the opportunity to continue your education and allows you to maintain a professional status in the community during your active participation. Of course, the job also provides you with an assistant to handle all the details of your employment and provides you with an accumulation of 90 to 180 days sick leave which can be taken at your discretion. If this sounds like an imaginary dream, think again. Most gang members in the United States enjoy the privileges that I've outlined above now. They view the negotiation process with the board of education as a give-away program. It is a one-sided give-away program in which periodically the gang asks for more benefits and in turn blackmails the board with a threatened withdrawal of services in the event that they do not capitulate to the demands of the organization. Most gang members today enjoy the ultimate position of security within a highly competitive structured salary system. They are secure from evaluation, they are secure from salary decreases, from the influence of inflation. In fact, they are secure from all of the threats that the normal working population of the country must face on a day to day basis. They are isolated from the real market of supply and demand. They have negotiated themselves into a privileged position in terms of the total working class of the U.S. Through a shattering devious procedure of manipulating popular opinion in favor of the negotiation process, the gang has traded the traditional reputation of teacher respect for a secure and self-serving package of individual teacher benefits which undermine the original purpose of the educational system and replace that purpose with a facsimile which can be described as teacher welfare.

Can you imagine a job which pays eighteen to twenty-six thousand dollars a year and has no meaningful evaluation process? Can you imagine not having your work evaluated by anyone? Or if it is evaluated by having the evaluation system so ineffective that all of the criticisms that are exposed cannot be remedied or enforcement of the remedies cannot take place. Such is the case with the teacher evaluation system. If a gang member is evaluated and that evaluation turns up a deficiency in performance, the evaluator has no way of enforcing that deficiency be corrected. Can you imagine a person who is a medical physician negotiating a salary which limits the amount of time that he treats patients? Such is the case in the teaching profession. More and more teachers are concerned with the amount of time that they are actually exposed to students. Their original purpose was to teach. The traditional professional teacher taught eight hours a day. Today's teacher is lucky to teach four actual hours of student contact. The other hours are divided up between preparation time, eating lunch, free periods, and so on and so on until effectively a school system is forced to hire twice as many teachers just in order to keep someone in the classroom. All this costs tax money. Can you imagine a job which allows you to negotiate the actual number of days you are going to work in a given year and which allows you each year to place pressure upon your employer which will force him to allow you to work less and less and less for more and more and more. Such is the case in education today. The gang has finally worked itself into a position where it can accumulate as many days sick leave as there are in a school year. If, for example, you can accumulate 180 days sick leave and if you are required to work only 180 days in a given year, then it is possible that you could take the entire year off due to some illness and be paid your normal contract rate which is 18 to 26 thousand dollars per year. Plus, in that situation, some systems allow you to continue to earn sick leave while you are on sick leave status. It's not uncommon to watch a superintendent who is supposed to be the head administrator in the school system call the president of the local gang and ask him what the policy interpretation is on sick leave accumulation or some other fringe benefit. In essence, the gang not only dictates system policy through the negotiation process, but they also play a majority role in terms of interpreting that policy after it has been negotiated. This is especially true if the negotiation process was difficult and resulted in the dismissal or resignation of a key administrator within the system. Every time the head administrator in a school system changes either for personal reasons or through political misfortune, the system, public, and the taxpayers lose strength in terms of enforcing the regulations of the system. The new administrator arrives on the scene unaware of all the events of the past. The ravenous leeches of the gang stand on the sidelines awaiting the arrival of the innocent lamb to the slaughter. Can you imagine a job in which you dictate to your employer the actual work that will be assigned to you? Such is the case in the gang and administration relationship. A senior gang member dictates to the administration that he wants an assignment which requires only one preparation per day. Take for example a school system that has two science teachers, one science teacher is required to teach only chemistry, the other science teacher must teach one section of chemistry, two sections of biology, two sections of general science, and a section of physics. The older teacher in the system demands that he be assigned to chemistry only, this means that he only prepares one class per day. A fair distribution of classes, of course, would be to divide the preparations among the two teachers so that each would have three preparations per day, but because of gang seniority, political position, and gang strength within the system, it is impossible to assign responsibilities in a fair and equal manner. Therefore, the new teacher coming into the system, is forced to take whatever the old gang members do not want in terms of assignments. The administrators are forced to place old gang members in favored positions and new gang members any place the old ones want them. This sets up an unusual situation within the system. For example, let's assume that there is a tenured gang member teaching Algebra II. Because the gang member only wants one preparation per day and there are only five sections of Algebra II, the gang member teaches all of the Algebra II classes. Let's assume further that this particular gang member is ineffective as a teacher and thus students are not learning Algebra II as they should. Let's assume third that Algebra II is a requirement for college preparation and thus all students in the school who want to go to college must take the course. We set up an entrapment situation whereby a student is forced to be exposed to an ineffective teacher. It's impossible for the student to take the course from another teacher because there is no one else in the system teaching the course. The teacher is absolutely ineffective in terms of teaching the course to the student, thus it is impossible to get the student around the teacher, thus we have a direct conflict that has been set up through the manipulation of the gang and the demands of the organization. The result of this conflict is not unusual, the student is unhappy, possibly fails the course, possibly is required to remediate the course the first year in college if he passes the entrance exam. Although this is a common situation, it is sometimes difficult for parents to understand why their child is not passing a particular course or worse, not learning a particular subject. It is possible that the child would pass the course because many ineffective, inefficient gang members pass students in order to gain political popularity within the student population. So old Mr. Roadblock could pass all of the students with high marks, yet not teach them the subject matter. In that situation the end result would be a student who would fail college entrance exams, but be able to boast of high grades in the subject matter area, which in itself is an educationally unsound dichotomy.

Thus, in effect, gang members should not be allowed to negotiate contract length or the amount of time that they are going to be exposed to students. It should be understood that they are going to be exposed to students because that is their main purpose in being a teacher. It should also be understood that fringe benefits are a privilege of being employed by a system which is satisfied with your work, not a demand that is met as a result of blackmailing the system by withdrawing services. Financial allocations within the system should be made on the basis of what serves the student best. Every expenditure within the system should be analyzed according to the direct value students receive from the expenditure. For example, if a student is given a textbook for a course, he receives something for the money spent on that textbook. However, if a teacher is sent to a workshop and a large amount of budget is expended to expose that teacher to the workshop and the teacher returns without any significant gain in ability or knowledge, then the expenditure is in large wasted because the student receives nothing from the tax dollar. If, in fact, every expenditure that is made within the school was judged based upon the direct value it had to students in terms of their education, many budgets throughout the United States would be greatly reduced or cut in half.

Every expenditure of funds within the school should be evaluated upon their direct benefit to students. It's ridiculous to evaluate expenditures with regard to a teacher's demands. A gang member can request a new coffee pot for the Home Economics department. Upon closer observation one finds that the coffee pot is being used for the gang meeting at the end of the day. Business Education teacher might request a new duplicating machine for instructional purposes. Upon closer observation one finds that the machine is being used to duplicate political propaganda for the organization. The entire athletic department decides that they need a new trampoline for instructional purposes and even requests a swimming pool to be built on the campus. A year later we find that the trampoline is not used for instructional purposes because of the injuries and danger involved, but that we have a staff member who has a hobby of exercising on a trampoline and that the rules and regulations governing the use of the swimming pool are so rigid that it's also impossible for a student to get wet. However, the regulations are flexible enough to allow the teachers organization to use the pool for any social activity which might be required. Such is the dichotomy which faces the taxpaying public. Wasteful expenditures are made every day for the purpose of strengthening the gang's political position, for making the hideout more comfortable, and for equipping the gang for the political wars of the future. Little or no consideration is given to the educational value of the expenditures nor the wasteful utilization of public funds. Only the gang and the welfare of gang members and the value of the expenditure for the gang is a reasonable consideration for any use of tax money. Students are secondary citizens of the school system. Their existence is maintained for the purpose of legitimizing the existence of the institution. Other than that, they are a necessary evil and useless to the cause of the organization.

How would you like to have a position where you could select your own boss? Such is the case with the gang. New administrators in the system are more and more being selected according to criteria developed by the gang. Of course, that criteria is political nonsense which is developed to justify the selection of a person who is sympathetic to the purposes of the gang. Once the person is selected, he is skillfully manipulated as a scapegoat for perpetuating the political goals of that particular gang unit. Examine the policies which control the selection of administrators and enforcers within your local institutions. Much to your surprise you will discover that these key positions are closely controlled by the gang philosophy. You will discover that rules and regulations have been adopted which were initiated by the gang for the purpose of eroding the control over gang members.

Remember, the prize is the complete and unconditional control of all financial and other resources of the educational institution by the gang and its membership. In other words, the educational system will be defeated when the administrators of the system in the person of the school administration and board of education, surrender to the gang or the teachers organization and/or its representatives all of the power or the majority of the power of control over financial and non-financial resources within the system. The prize is to be able to spend taxpayers money for any purpose for which the gang feels it can justify to the taxpaying public the expenditure. By inculcating the expenditure in educational terminology and manipulation, the gang can successfully spend any amount of money for any purpose and justify it to the taxpaying public. Although this seems clever it is in fact dishonest and against the foundation of our democratic system.

Let's look at some of the situations which the gang have currently manipulated in their favor. At one time it was thought to be an educational advantage to have speech therapists, special education personnel, hearing therapists, vocational education teachers, and other specialists including counselors and school psychologists on the staff. That situation originated because it was felt that specialized knowledge would help bring about a better educational system and in effect satisfy the needs of students to a higher degree. Most schools are required by local gangs in order to increase the number of gang members within a particular institution justify employing more gang members and decreasing the work load of the existing gang members by watering down the number of students each teacher was required to be exposed. Most systems now require that any newly created positions or vacant positions within the school system be advertised among the current staff members with seniority within the system and allow them to take advantage of newly created positions. Now it has become a method for staff members to move who they desire to have in the system for political reasons and to ensure that none will be brought into the system unless they have gang approval.

Most gangs have negotiated into their contracts a phrase relating to member evaluation which reads "contractually defined evaluation procedures", this actually means that the contract that the gang member receives must include an evaluation procedure approved by that particular member. Of course, no member will approve a procedure for evaluating his performance which would jeopardize his employment. Therefore, all of the evaluation procedures used within the system allow the individual several chances for improving his performance or at least justifying it in such a way that no action can be taken against him regardless of how revolting the performance might be. Another phrase negotiated in most contracts reads "enforcable class size and teaching load maximums". This phrase simply means that the individual gang member dictates exactly what his class size will be, whether he will have fifteen students, twenty students, twenty-five students, and how many classes each day he will have, and how many different subject matters he will be responsible for teaching. This is another way that the individual gang member regulates the amount of time the system has him on call. If the gang member is effective in his negotiation procedure, the system will have him on call very little and he will be able to spend more time on gang activities. Thus, the gang member once again rewards himself with the prize of little or no work or responsibility in return for maximum salary and fringe benefits. In effect, once he has developed a strong position after negotiations, he is able to work virtually as he desires, at whatever he desires, and reserve the remainder of his time for anything that he desires. This in itself is a great prize and achievement and the organization is likely to consider him extremely successful if he has been able to secure such a position within the system. He will be envied among the younger staff members.

Administrative personnel selection has always traditionally been the responsibility of the board of education and/or selected administrators within the school system. For example, the board normally delegates the selection of principals and assistant principals in the system to the chief school administrator who is usually the superintendent of schools. The superintendent then delegates the selection of quasi administrative personnel to the actual administrators for whom they would work on a daily basis. The situation has changed radically throughout the system as a result of gang influence. The gang now voices an opinion with regard to any administrative selection. The questionnaire, of course, has been developed by the gang for the purpose of limiting the choices to gang sympathizers. Once the administrator is selected, the gang then uses his answers to the questionnaire as criteria for limiting his decision making. For example, if he asked on the questionnaire what his position with regard to teacher evaluation would be and he answers that he would be very liberal and use every technique available to ensure that a teacher had the opportunity to remediate his efforts, and then in turn was hired and followed a policy contrary to that indicated on the questionnaire, the teachers organization would be quick to remind him of his position with regard to that matter before his selection as an administrator in the district. Thus the circle is complete and administrators are sanc-

THE PRIZE

tioned and controlled by the teachers who work directly for them. This of course creates an ideal climate in which the gang members can take major advantage of the entire system of which they are a part. Can you imagine a position where you are guaranteed preparation time, planning time, and completely duty free lunch periods? This is the current situation in most school districts. Not only do the gang members limit through their contract negotiations the amount of time that they are actually exposed to students roughly about four 30-minute periods for a total of two hours per day, but they also require through their negotiations that they have adequate time for preparation for each of those 30-minute periods that they are exposed to students, normally they expect at least an equal amount of time for preparation thus, a 30-minute period in the classroom requires 30-minute preparation outside the classroom. Of course, that preparation time is not always used for its intended purpose, in fact, it is usually not used. Therefore, most teachers teach 30 minutes, have a 30-minute preparation period, teach another 30 minutes, have a 30 to 45-minute lunch period, possibly another 30-minute preparation period, then their day is complete, thus, the effect is that they have much free time during the school day to use in planning and developing political strategies for the gang membership.

In the old days when teachers were dedicated and concerned about their professionalism, they carried out the educational process with dignity and effectiveness. If an administrator disagreed with a teacher's approach in the classroom, he discussed it with that teacher in a professional manner and they arrived at a compromise which both were satisfied with. As a result, there were very few grievances in the school system that could not be totally satisfied to everyone's opinion. In the modern system gang members have changed all of that. Today there is a grievance procedure which outlines in a very legalistic manner how all criticisms of any gang member will be handled. The gang has founded a foolproof procedure based upon arbitration which forces an administrator to follow very rigid guidelines in the process of criticizing a teacher's function. The guidelines not only limit the administrator as to what he may criticize, but they also limit the amount of time which he has to solve the problem. As a result, if the administrator becomes adamant about his position with regard to any given matter, the administrator is effectively isolated through an arbitration agreement with the board of education, so that in effect he does not have the power to make the final decision with regard to how the teacher will behave in the classroom. Thus, it is possible for a teacher who is tenured (completed three years of successful teaching and been approved by tenure by the board of education) he or she can do virtually anything they like within the classroom and the most radical repercussion the gang member will suffer is a subjection to arbitration procedure. This procedure will end up in binding arbitration which will in effect nullify any type of administrative control over the individual. Another aspect of the same problem involves the reduction of services within a school system. For example, if a local community rebels at the amount of taxes being paid to support the schools, and as a result the school budget is cut, then of course it follows that some personnel must be eliminated throughout the system. In the days of traditional education those limitations were made based upon the merits of the individual teachers involved. For example, if a school system was forced to limit the number of teachers on the staff by three or four, and there were three or four weak teachers who had been evaluated by administrative personnel and found to be deficient in the classroom, they would have, of course, been the first to be cut. However, today gang members are protected from this sort of reduction. If an administrator is forced to reduce, his total staff by five teachers, he must reduce it in accordance with seniority within the system. In other words, the youngest teachers or the newest teachers in the system would be cut first, not the poorest teachers. As a result, a very poor teacher who has seniority within the system could end up being the last teacher in the system to lose his position. This in effect has greatly reduced the administrator's latitude with regard to weeding out undesirables within the system. Once again, this becomes a prize for participation in the gang mania.

Another favorite target of gang

THE PRIZE

members is class size. This simply means the number of students a gang member must meet with in each class. Gang members, of course, dislike large numbers of students because this requires unique ability in the teaching process. If a gang member can position himself with three or four 30-minute classes and then at the same time limit the number of students in those classes to 20 or 25 students, then he has effectively won another prize which is his limited contact with students and the limited amount of time he is exposed to a limited number of students. This is a wonderful prize for a gang member, since once he has effectively limited the number of students which can attend any given class, he is in a position to select students for that class, thus he has the perogative of turning down students who want to take the course based upon their past behavioral patterns or opinions of his teaching ability. Once again, the popularity contest rules supreme and the gang member has another lever to use with regard to influencing students to support his classroom manner. As you can see, with administrators tied up in the red tape of trying to understand a lengthy involved negotiated contract, with teachers who in turn are doing everything politically possible to force interpretations in their favor, he has little time to effectively supervise the learning process. Once he is effectively neutralized through this mass political attack upon the power structure, the gang is in a position to dictate exactly their role within the system. Armed with the financial position of the system as well as all of the resources which were originally directed toward the educational process, the gang is now in a position to take full advantage of the political opportunities which exist as a result of their efforts. The prizes rule supreme. They can gain complete political control over the educational process. They can dictate their own time schedule within the system. They can effectively limit the number of students that they must expose themselves to. They can effectively limit the number of minutes that they are tied down during the day thus making more time for their political shenanigans. In effect, the gang members can do what they like, when they like within the school system with very little interference from the chain of command and/or the power structure which is supposed to be effectively directing the system. They can buy new equipment and fund political projects designed to fortify their political positions and goals within the system. They can even design buildings to make it more effective for the type of group political efforts that they have built into their overall objectives. The organizational structure of the system can be modified to better serve their political purposes. Gradually over a period of time the administration is so undermined and the board of education is so neutralized that the system is completely in control of the gang. A popularity contest runs supreme throughout the system constantly reinforcing student behavior in favor of teacher behavior. Gradually the organization wins the prize of community support through the popularity contest directed at both students and parents. In effect, the total prize is the total control and use of the system and its resources. Once this is accomplished, the gang can carry the head of the system to the regional and state meetings claiming victory on all levels. The complete prostitution of control within the system means the supreme victory for the gang. To the victor go the spoils. And in the school business the spoils means complete control over facilities, equipment, and personnel within the school system. Budgets are altered to serve the purpose of the organization. Personnel can be hired and recruited and dictated by the gang for the purpose of the gang. If a gang happens to be weak in a given area and knows of a gang member in another district, they can have that gang member recruited as a teacher in their district, thus bringing in reinforced professional gang mentality into their own system. All this political manipulation and undermining takes place in a well-equipped comfortable environment. With gang members well in charge of all the prizes that they have designed as their political objectives. Once control is complete, the gang member rests assured that he will retire with full benefits, that he cannot be dismissed from his job for any reason, and that he has secured a politically well defined and favorable position within the district and the community. He can rest assured that he has the power to perpetuate the increases of taxes to support his own political motives. He can rest assured that he can elect leaders within the community and appoint administrators and other supervisory personnel within the system who will be sympathetic to his goals and methods. He knows that he is secure in an environment that he has created through his own wisdom and ability to manipulate a complex system of taxes and indirect control. Once the gang member has reached this level of total realization of power within the district, he is a threat to all who do not agree with his objectives. He can have people moved in and out of positions within the district at will. He can spend money that was budgeted for education for any purpose which he desires. He can freely and without mercy attack the unsuspecting taxpayer and the innocent and naive student body. He can continue to build his popularity among students and have them carry that popularity to their taxpaying parents in an effort to continue to fund his existence. He becomes a total threat and leech upon public resources. He has reached nirvana in terms of his perpetuating his own existence. Once his lecherous existence is secure, he can direct himself at building an army of leeches or a gang of loyal members. As they bleed the system of all which is reasonable and educational, they thrive in knowing that this is their ultimate prize, an escape from their responsibility as professionals into the dark morass of political indignation within their appointed function as they define it. Gang wisdom rules supreme and all those who defy it perish. Gang leaders rule supreme and all those who defy their dictatorial approach to the control of resources and personnel perish under their sword of injustice and political manipulation. Gang welfare rules supreme and institutional welfare perishes in the smoke of political disorder. All inefficiency within the normal structure of the system disappears under the murky waters of political favoritism and popularity. If the power to control one's destiny is not enough of a prize, then consider the power to control not only the destiny of the gang, but the destiny of the institution which has allowed the gang to develop, and the destiny of the society which depends upon the gang's professionalism. All of this is the prize. All of this is the goal of a successful gang member and the unit of which he is a part. Success breeds success and gang success breeds gang success. As the strength of the gang increases, the goals and objectives increase and the appetite for more political disorder, corruption, and influence over the total institution increases. Just as greed fuels the fires of corruptibility, so does gang greed and appetite fuel the fires for further political subterfuge greed. On and on into the annals of the institution, the gang continues to breed corruption and influence and thus destroys all good and all which is educational. Its success that thrives on the misuse of the institution and thus the usefulness of the institution and the purpose of the institution are destined to misuse and destruction.

CHAPTER VII

THE VICTIMS

Who are the victims of this crime? Of course the children. The children who cannot protect themselves from the substructure of the system. The children who are innocent and are entrapped by the system. The children who cannot evaluate the system which they are forced to participate in. The children that we send to the school for the purpose of education but who receive a series of artificial experiences designed to develop loyalty and favoritism toward teachers. The children who we know do not have the experience nor the ability to evaluate their education progress yet are naive enough to want an easy path to follow. The children who are corrupted and tempted by an easy system which requires only that they support those who are in charge and reward the inefficient system with their loyalty and ver-

THE VICTIMS

bal praise. The children who are being robbed of their right to a formal education in a free society according to their ability as it is nutured and developed by a sound educational system. The children are certainly the victims of the misuse of educational funds and facilities for the political purpose of a subversive organization. The gang gains strength on the blood of its victims. The children are innocent and naive as they are being robbed of their future and of their right under a free system to receive a formal education. The robbery is evident from the performance of the children. Every year seniors are graduated from high school who cannot read. These are the victims. These are the sacrificial lambs of an unmerciful substructure which has developed into a cancer undermining the entire purpose of education in the U. S.

Children, of course, should be cheerful and should appreciate the plush surroundings and tapestry of an educational system no longer directed toward their service. They cannot be expected to repel an attack from a power structure aimed at their destruction. They realize that they are not learning but they cannot be expected to understand why the system does not produce the product it was intended to. They are told by gang members that more equipment is needed, that more funds are needed, that they must work harder to develop themselves. All the time the gang members realize that it is their misuse of funds, misuse of facilities and waste of student time that results in the failure to produce the type of education that the children should receive for the price that is being paid. Truly the children expect a quality education for the time and effort that they spend in the classroom. However, they are caught in the quicksand of meaningless lessons, wasted time, poor teacher planning and busy work, all continued under the guise of education. Gang members present to them daily outmoded, outdated and useless subject matter. Gang members thrust upon them their own biases and uselessness. Children are innocent and naive, they believe that school should be fun. The gang members use this ploy to entice them into entertainment within the classroom. Gang members major in entertainment and popularity, fun not work, freedom not discipline. As a result, morals decay, education is submerged in the muck of politics, and the children are robbed. Without discipline in the classroom, there is no respect for the system, and without respect for the system, there is no purpose nor motivation to satisfy the rigid demands of formal education. Who should supply the discipline within the school? Should the gang or should the children? Of course, children cannot be expected to provide their own direction through the maze of formal education which is required to prepare a child to be an adult. How can we expect conscientious, contributing citizens in our society when they are prepared in a shoddy, makeshift, informal, undisciplined manner.

How can we expect children to learn when they are never given the correct answers. When they are asked to grade each others papers not knowing which answer is correct, when they are never evaluated properly, when they are given general evaluations such as satisfactory or unsatisfactory, and when they are asked to replace learning with popularity as a goal. Children enter the system as an unfilled pitcher. They are supposed to leave the system filled with an appreciation of knowledge and a desire to learn. Instead, they leave the system with a feeling that they have been exposed to a few popular teachers and have participated in a few entertaining and recreational experiences. Based upon their exposure to entertainment within the classroom and recreation outside the classroom, they are expected to enter the mainstream of adult life prepared to satisfy the pressures and responsibilities of citizenship in a free and growing country. It is no wonder that social conditions in the U. S. have deteriorated to the present status. It is amazing that the country is still within reasonable control.

A philosopher once said that at harvest time you reap what you sow. Just as in gardening, when you sow corn you reap corn not pumpkins or tomatoes. The same is true in the classroom. If you sow shoddy performance, entertainment and recreation, you reap instability, lack of character and misfortune. Once these qualities are magnified and transferred into the mainstream of American life, the results are phenomenal. The basic population no longer is responsible, thus the system cannot derive good direction from

THE VICTIMS

a voting populous. Once the situation deteriorates to the point that citizens do not have the ability nor the knowledge to make adequate choices for themselves nor for the society of which they are a part, the end result must be deterioration of the society culminating in the destruction of the individual. Thus, the gang perpetuates the gang mentality which eroded the system of education within the U.S. The same gang mentality that was responsible for undermining the resources and facilities which were designed to perpetuate the system, now undermines the very purpose of those resources and facilities which is the country itself. Those children who learn in the classroom that they can survive in the system by praising the teachers who are in charge of them, learn at the same time that this is a solution to life. Much to their surprise, the real world requires more than praising one's superiors. Thus, as the learner reaches the real world, he is amazed to find that he is ill-equipped and unprepared to meet the challenges of life. He then retreats to the ways that he has learned, which are to entertain himself with recreational and free thinking in order to escape discipline, respect for the system, and the fundamental knowledge which equips one to participate in the normal problems which life presents.

How can the child learn or the citizen be prepared when they are constantly subjected to unfair politically oriented controls within the classroom? When the gang uses poor materials, poor curricular offerings, and presents the learner with poor alternatives which breed an evaluation which is misleading, the child doesn't have a chance. He is destined to be robbed not only of his present right to learn, but also of his future right to be equipped to contend with the obstacles and challenges of a hectic, fast-moving world. He can't expect to compete in higher education when he has never learned to study. He can't expect to compete for responsible positions in industry when he has never developed self discipline nor even been exposed to external discipline with success. He can be expected to understand welfare since he has learned to take anything which is given to him without remorse or self pity. He can't be expected to strive for perfectionism when he has never learned to be proud. Thus, when the gang robs the child of his natural ability, he robs the

THE VICTIMS

child of all the pleasure of being successful. Without success, the child feels failure, and just as success breeds success, so does failure breed failure. After the child fails a few times, it is easy to accept failure. The gang prepares the child to fail. Once the seed of failure is planted, the rewards of failure will be reaped. The gang is successful.

The child is trained by the gang to survive in an artificial environment called education. The child is exposed to the gang for twelve years and at that time he is supposed to be prepared to survive in a real non-artificial world. However, as one would expect, although the child is successful in surviving in the artificial world of the gang, he is not prepared to swim in the ocean of society. It's as if he was trained in a bathtub to swim the English Channel. Although it is ridiculous, it is true that the system allows gang cancer to erode the integrity of the process. If the children are fortunate, the gang only robs their opportunity. But for the less fortunate, the gang leaves them barren without hope. They are robbed of their own self respect, of their respect for the system, of their own dignity, of their individuality, and of every other trait which we attach to a successful individual. They are completely patronized and prostituted to the will and the means of the gang. Without mercy they are raped by the system. The children are robbed on all levels, the gang is unmerciful. They are robbed in the classroom, in the hallways, in the extra-curricular programs, and in the minds of their peers. Although they cry for help, their words go unheard. The system does not listen to children. The system listens to the gang. The gang has the power to persuade the system to listen, the children are powerless, their cries are unmerciful yet they fall on deaf ears. Everyone knows that children cannot determine their own destiny. They are shaped and molded by those who are responsible. In the school system the Robbers are responsible.

Actually when the gang robs children of their right to free public education, they commit a major crime against the child and the society. Robbing one of his natural ability to prosper in a free system is roughly equivalent to committing assassination. What is the difference between killing a child and killing his mind? When a child puts his trust and faith in a teacher

THE VICTIMS

to mold his ability so that he might survive in a complex society, and that trust and faith is breached by a logical cunning mind, is this not equivalent to destroying the child? One could contend that the gang robs the child in such a way that a tangible illustration could be hanging. In other words, if a gang member would hang your child, would he do more harm than misleading that child in the educational process?

Of course not only the child is robbed. Parents lose the money that they pay into the system for education. The children, of course, lose the opportunity to be exposed to the educational process in the traditional definition. The community loses the values which tradition has taught us are necessary to produce a stable society. As those values are eroded, the community loses the opportunity to appreciate the support of the citizens it produces. The country as a whole loses the stability of a population with common values. Without common values each segregated group within the society goes its own way according to its individual leadership. This fragments the total purpose of our society and direction of our country. Without common direction there is no growth nor control. Gradually the public rebels first in groups which try to sway the population toward their individual purposes, and then later the groups band together in an effort to force a selected set of values upon a larger segment of the population. The schools and the system lose public confidence and thus public support. The teaching profession loses its respect and position within the society. The administration of the school loses the respect of its staff and eventually of the community. In general, the system of education loses its total reputation.

Within the system the curriculum quality is greatly diminished. Knowledge is lost to generalism and inefficiency. National achievement stops and national growth is terminated. The democratic system no longer functions since the democratic process has been eroded and replaced with an autocratic single purpose gang. All this culminates in robbing the society of a way of life which has produced one of the greatest countries in the world. Basic skills such as reading, writing and arithmetic are lost to general abilities such as watching television, entertaining ones self with degraded morals, and a replacement of earning potential with welfare programs. Accountability throughout the system of education and the system of government gives way to a low credibility standard. Teacher confidence is completely destroyed. The child in the system is robbed of the value of independent thinking. If the individual is not taught by the system to think independently according to a moral value structure, then direction and purpose throughout the society is lost. Money is wasted as the system gradually weakens. Local control gives way to state and federal mandate. Local financing is lost to federally controlled money. All look to the federal government for leadership out of the quicksand of system decay.

The gang succeeds. The children are destroyed. The purpose of the gang grows stronger and the influence over the society increases. Gradually the social structure which originally developed a strong nation is lost. All become dependent on centralized control over funds and resources. Everyone looks for leadership to guide them back to old traditions and values. Religion rises as a crutch for all who need help. In general the entire system as we have traditionally known it is destroyed.

In an effort to cover over their activities the gang becomes more and more involved in a public relations campaign aimed at selling education. The selling process is designed to convince people that education still exists. All energies and resources are directed toward convincing the taxpaying population that education is still intact and that children are still learning. In fact, knowledge and traditional education is replaced by a sophisticated public relations effort by the gang. The gang becomes more and more powerful and uses that power to further distort the real purpose of education. The system is raped and the children are hung. The children are robbed and destroyed by the gang which seeks power beyond imagination. The appetite for control is impossible to satisfy. Slowly the gang completely erodes both the system, the community, and the country. All that is left is a shell of what was once a productive society. Children no longer have marketable skills. They can no longer be part of the work force. They can only look to central authority for handouts in the form of welfare and

THE VICTIMS

unemployment payments.

As the system discovers that it is being used in the most vicious sense of the word, it tries to regain the old traditional values by attacking those who have destroyed it. Gradually the system realizes the gang is the enemy. But the enemy has grown so strong and the system so weak that the conflict is minimal. At this point the robbers can only continue to rob and the victims can only continue to be victimized. The system no longer has the strength to fight back. The shell of the giant collapses under the erosion and power of the gang. The children are robbed of their very existence. They are robbed of their contribution. And they are robbed of their livelihood. All that is left is to be dependent upon the leeches. While the coffers of resources of public funds are overflowing from tax dollars, the system and the children starve for the knowledge they need to survive.

Can there be any greater crime against society than to rob the young of their opportunity to learn? Even the Romans who enslaved the Hebrewonites allowed the young to participate as slaves in the society. Genghis Khan conquered all of Persia yet never denied the young of education. During the Third Reich, Hitler distorted the values of a society and prostituted a system to his own will, yet even though he and his system created atrocities beyond belief, never did he purge the system of its right to survive. Black slavery in the U.S. allowed the young to become a replacement for their parents. Although organized vice in the U.S. today distorts the values of the young and corrupts their minds, at least they allow them the opportunity to learn right from wrong. All of the great crimes against society ranging from the Romans to Watergate have never directed their purges toward the youth which would perpetuate the actual existence of the society. Most revolutions have looked to the young as the vehicle for perpetuation of the new system. The young are always educated to carry on the new traditions and the new ideas. Revolution starts in the school. In our system, however, the opposite is taking place. Instead of educating the young to start a new morality and thrive in the sunlight of a new ordeal, we are depriving them of the opportunity to learn what is necessary to survive. Thus,

THE VICTIMS

truly, our children are being robbed. And that robbery is in progress now.

CHAPTER VIII

THE COPS

Who watches the store? Who has both the authority and responsibility for policing a school system? Who has the ultimate responsibility for assuring that the gang lives up to their commitments? The board of education is an elected body of private citizens. They are not usually schooled as educators. However, they all have an interest in the schools and in most cases have children in the schools. Of course, the logical reasoning indicates that if a person has a child in the schools and is concerned with that child's welfare and education, that he in fact would be concerned with the institution which provides that education for the child. Interpreted, this means that the individual school board member is most interested in that aspect of the school which serves his children. This point can be emphasized by the fact that when most school boards are forced to reduce educational programs, that they look first to those educational programs which will not affect their individual children in the school. Of course, this is a natural inclination and is somewhat offset by the fact that different board members have children interested in different academic programs throughout the school which tends to nullify the bias. School board members also are responsible for financial allocations within the school. They approve the annual budget and any special expenditures which are not included in the annual budget. As taxpayers, you would assume that school board members would be careful and thorough in their analysis of the expenditures presented to them for approval. But, in fact, just as school board members are not educated as teachers, most of them also are not educated as accountants. As a school system becomes larger and more complex, the budget becomes larger and more difficult to understand. Of course there are always superficial questions and of course there's much checking and debate about individual budget items. However, in the last analysis, it's necessary for school board members to take the advice and counsel of both the administration and teaching staff since they do not have the inside expertise nor time to analyze sufficiently the gross complex of expenditures which are necessary to keep the system operating. Board members are a peculiar breed. They spend endless hours in meetings discussing the merits of various educational systems and programs. They spend endless hours discussing financial problems within the district. They spend endless hours trying to understand recently enacted laws governing both the student body and the instructional program. At best, most of them are equipped to analyze these complex problems only to the degree of their individual formal educational specialization. For example, if a lawyer is a board member, then it's possible that he would understand the legal aspects of the school problems. If an M.D. is a board member, of course he would understand the health problems associated and all would understand to some degree all of the problems associated with the school. However, it is rare to find a board member that possesses expertise and knowledge in all areas which confront him upon the board. Therein lies the Achilles heel of the board and the obvious potential for error.

Boards of education are elected not appointed. This simply means that they represent the people. They have a constituency. And they serve that constituency. How accurately do boards of education represent the people? Upon close analysis one realizes that there are many reasons to become a board member. Some board members consider their position as a stepping stone to a political future which involves running for higher office. Some board members consider the board of education a platform upon which they may gain popularity, praise, and recognition within a community. Take for example a local optometrist or veterinarian. These individuals have spent several years of their life educating themselves in a profession. Upon entering the profession they realize that they receive very little or no social recognition for their efforts. In order to enhance their position in the community they run for the school board. Once upon the board their picture appears in the paper several times a year and their position in the community as an authority both in their professional field and in education is promoted. If a person has an ego need, being a school board member can somewhat satisfy it. In fact the position as school board member places many individuals in a power position which they would rarely have the opportunity to be exposed to if it were not for their position on the board. This simply means that school board members run for the school board for various social and personal reasons which are not necessarily related to the pursuit of better educational programs for the community in which they serve. One of the most frequent reasons for school board members to run for the board is simply to grind an axe. By this I mean seek out a teacher within the district that for some reason they are unhappy with and pursue a course which will ultimately destroy that individual. Many school board members run for the board to fire a teacher. Of course they are naive about the complexities involved in achieving that task. Once they find themselves on the board they realize that there exists a holocaust of issues which must be satisfied before the board is free to concentrate upon a problem which serves the individual purpose of a singular board member. Thus, the newly elected board member thinking the first week he attends a board meeting he will be able to accomplish his goal and rid the system of an undesirable teacher who failed his child, finds instead that his time will be spent analyzing endless forms and paraphernalia used in the process of education within the district, handling endless grievances from parents within the district, and probably answering his personal telephone at home many evenings trying to pacify parents who are upset with both the administration, the school board and the teaching staff. All of these things take priority over his original purpose for running for the board.

Another aspect of boardmanship is his responsibility to represent the employees within the school district. This means he must represent both teachers and non-teaching employees. Remember he always represents the taxpaying public and the students in the district, not to mention the administration which he is responsible for hiring and evaluating. If it's not obvious, it should be, that there is a direct and constant conflict of loyalties between all of these bodies. Therefore, the board member becomes an arbiter, constantly working out compromise positions between all the political factions that he represents. This position, of course, is overlaid on top of the administrative details that he must oversee. The conscientious board member thus spends hours and hours and hours of research within the district talking to taxpayers, students, teachers, administrators, other board members, and concerned citizens about all of the factors which make up the entire district. He tries to understand and apply the laws which have been issued by the various legislators and formed into statutes which he must attempt to adhere. He attempts to plot a fair and reasonable and prudent course in the process of hiring, firing, setting salaries, and listening to the various grievances and complaints throughout the system. He tries to establish in his own mind with the help of his counsel in the person of administrators and others, concerned priorities for the entire system in each area of complication. He is on constant alert and emergency call to put out fires within the system. For example, an enraged parent calls him at midnight complaining that her daughter recently failed an algebra test and as a result will have difficulty being admitted to college. The alert board member, of course, takes the problem to heart, immediately calls an administrator or worse the teacher involved, and pursues the problem as a knight on a white horse. In most cases, the entire situation ends up in total disaster and the child is the most embarrassed. Usually, if the board member had ignored the situation, the child would have worked harder the next six-week period and passed the course. Nothing more needs to be said about over-reaction. It is a constant plague of every administrator who ever walked into a school.

Thus, we must realize with all of the responsibility and pressures upon the board members, with all of the inexperience and insecurity among members, and with the constant turnover of members and the pressure of personal responsibilities which take them away from their duties as school board members, it is impossible for a member to be prepared at all times for all things for everyone in the system. Thus, the school board becomes a cautious, conservative, slow-moving legislative group reacting to proposals from all sources within the district which require meditation, concentration, and thorough research on the part of each member in order to make wise, prudent, consistent decisions which govern a system. In this climate of slow-moving conservative thought, is it any wonder that the school board is no match for the gang. The gang is a fast-moving, quick to react, first hand knowledge, immediate, isolated situation oriented organization. It is equipped as a light cavalry, can rush in, bring many resources to bear on a given situation quickly and conquer the situation or force it in the direction it chooses. The school board, on the other hand, is like a huge battleship without power. It sets there with its big guns pointing in all directions waiting to be blown out of the water. In most cases, when it fires its big guns, it either overshoots the target because it can't possibly move fast enough to aim the gun in the right direction, or it just burns up money and energy by firing the shells. While the teachers organization is running around the ship doing everything possible to sink it, the board sits there in the water unable to focus its guns down to its sides where gashing holes are being ripped and water is flowing. In essence, one might say that the school board is unprepared, outnumbered, and designed in such a way that it is impossible for it to cope with the problems at hand. It is slow to react, it is conservative to react, it needs information to react, and the gathering of accurate, complete information from unbiased sources is difficult and time consuming. The school board is poorly equipped in an age of computer technology, most board members are fortunate to have the use of a paper tablet and pencil. They lack the specialized background in areas of curriculum. This makes it easy for experienced, knowledgeable educators to completely confuse them on all fronts. As a result, they approve expenditures on curriculum proposals which have little or no merit. They accept educational jargon and buzz words as being gospel when they are the creation of some imagination in education. They listen to grandiose schemes and calculated statistics aimed at convincing them that the course is right and fair and true, when in fact, the statistics are misleading, the individuals promoting the program are more interested in self-indulgence, and in fact the program has little or no educational significance. As a result of this lack of background, funds are wasted, time is wasted, and educators are allowed to escape their primary responsibilities for teaching within the system. In spite of all these problems, school board members still maintain their prestige as the ultimate authority within the district. That prestige alone becomes another millstone tied to their neck. Board members are patronized by everyone in the system. They are coddled to, they are impressed by, in fact they are manipulated in every possible way by both administrators, teachers, students, parents, and all others concerned with the general direction of the educational process. Once again, rarely do they have the political awareness nor experience to cope with this type of subterfuge. They lack the political background and awareness to know when they are being patronized. And in fact, it is impossible for them to control their own political destiny within the system.

In spite of all of this, board members attempt to do the job of policing the system. How can they police the gang when their own board security has been violated and infiltrated? In many, many cases throughout the country teachers have strategically placed hand-picked board members upon the board who routinely report every significant word which is spoken at a board meeting back to the gang. The gang thus knows everything that is happening on the board and in the system virtually before it takes place. It is impossible for a board to handle the complexed personal problems of teacher control when they cannot maintain security among five, seven, or nine members of the board. When every bit of significant information which is shared with the board by administrators is distorted and reported back to the organization by an inside board member who has the added advantage of being able to discuss the individual teacher in question with other board members and thus reporting back to the gang a composite opinion, in many cases before the administrator in charge of the situation has an opportunity to understand the board's composite view on the subject. With this insecurity, this lack of continuity of purpose, this lack of integrity between the controlling bodies within the system, it is impossible to control the organization. The gang runs rampant and has a field day by playing politics internally with the board. In fact, the gang advises and counsels board members in their pursuit of purpose among the other members. For example, a board member working for the gang, elected by the gang, is supporting an individual teacher who is being reprimanded by the administration. In order to win the political battle the board member seeks counsel and advice from the teachers organization. Thus, the stage is set. The board member under the advice of the gang is fighting for a gang member's survival. He is fighting for that survival against four or five other board members and the administration. At the same time he is in a position to demand the respect and security and confidence of the administration and other members that he opposes. Since the other members of the board and the administration are unaware of his loyalty to the gang, he is able to successfully provide the gang with accurate, complete detailed information concerning the gang member situation. With this type of situation it is impossible for the administration and other board members to successfully confront individual gang members with personal problems which endanger the success and education within the system. As with all of us, board members have various degrees of personal insecurity and paranoia. Most board members hesitate to take a frontal attack when problems are presented to them. Of course they want what's right for the system, but are they willing to take a strong political stand which might end up costing them their reputation in the community if in fact they are wrong. Most board members do not have this type of confidence and ability. In turn they walk the line trying to find out which side is right, which side is wrong, their ultimate position is to bring peace to the system with the least amount of effort. Most board members want things to run smoothly, therefore, they are not willing to start conflict, even when conflict is needed within the system to rid the system of undesirable elements. Most board members do not have the security of purpose and self-confidence to attack a problem frontally and destroy the ineffectiveness within the system regardless of what the cost. Most board members want the administration to solve the problem and solve it with the least amount of difficulty and that means keeping board members out of it. Most board members do not want to take a position which will put them in the spotlight in terms of explaining the complications within the system to the public. They would rather use an administrator to explain the complexities of the system, and then if he is not successful or the public refuses to accept the situation, they would rather dismiss the administrator and replace him, thus using him as a scapegoat for the problem, than they would solve the problem and return the educational system of the community to its rightful level of prestige and effectiveness. Thus, is it any wonder that in the sad situation where the board and administration is completely outnumbered by a gang who is well organized and effective in circumventing, undermining, and infiltrating the powers that be, that there is no match. It is impossible for the cops to control the robbers. The cops try, but the robbers are too swift and effective.

The system must go on. Thus, the

THE COPS

outnumbered administration and board trudges daily through the complexities and involvements of the system. Repeatedly the board loses battles. The thought is as long as the war goes on, one can lose battles. The real situation is that the board holds the position of power, but the gang holds the actual power and authority within the school system. That the board makes the rules but the board cannot enforce the rules, the board makes the regulations and the gang interprets those regulations to their satisfaction. Where there is a conflict between the gang and board's representative, which is the administrator in the system, either the administrator decides an interpretation of the regulation in the gang's favor, or he is destroyed through character assassination by the gang and replaced by the board. Thus, confidence and efficiency and effectiveness in education gives way to pressure, politics, and gang authority. Since the gang is gradually achieving all the goals that it has set out for itself, rather than change the system it works methodically behind the scene to see to it that the board survives. In other words, the gang helps the board blame the administration for any problems or situations which have not been effectively resolved, thus, the gang cleverly replaces administrators and preserves the board, since the board is not blamed for anything that goes wrong within the system, the board's integrity and popularity is preserved and they are grateful to the gang. The gang in turn expects additional favors from the board as repayment for helping them survive. The circle is complete, board members win, gang members win, administrators lose. Administrators then become the fall points to the system. Anything that goes wrong in the system must be an administrator's fault. Since administrators are usually short-term participants in the process of education within a community, since they are periodically assassinated by the gang and board, they are not deeply embedded in the social structure, and their prestige and ability can be reconstituted in another community for a short period of time. Thus, administrators survive by moving from district to district every two or three years and once again play out the role of the eternal scapegoat. Regardless of how sincere their motives, how well prepared they are professionally, or their concern with the welfare of the system, eventually they will end up on the scrap heap of scapegoats and martyrs. In fact, if we see them on the field of battle as three opposing teams, the board member encompasses the power and authority through the election to the board, the teachers of course represent a large body of soldiers who are willing to sacrifice themselves in any way to preserve the group, the administrator stands alone with only his training, knowledge, expertise and natural ability to survive in an alley fight to fend off both the authority of the board and the numbers of the teachers attacking the system. He becomes a singular knight in shining armor riding his white horse off in all directions at the same time. The board and the teacher has only one answer for financial problems within the system. That answer is to ask the public taxpayers for more money. Administrators try to carve down the budget and run the system efficiently. Teachers argue that if they cannot have a well-equipped system with the supplies and programs that they demand, it is impossible for them to provide adequate education. Thus, out of fear that the educational system is going to be inadequate, the board agrees to buy the materials and equipment needed to fund the program. As a result, the budget is exceeded and the board is forced to ask for more money. The teachers are not opposed to this so they support the board in the contention that the taxpayers are not paying enough for quality education. The taxpayers are then blamed because they demand too much of the system and the administrator is left in the middle looking very inefficient and ineffective. As a result, the board asks the taxpayers for money, the taxpayers pay the money, the teachers waste the money, and the administration is once again blamed for the waste. The most experienced and capable school administrator in the world can only hope to lengthen his survival time, his ultimate destiny is predetermined. He will be sacrificed upon the pile of wasted scapegoats. He can temporarily offset his destiny by being effective, efficient and gradually giving in to the demands of the board and gang. He can never hope to continually survive, since each time he sacrifices efficient and effective operation of the system to political whim and power, he gradually

THE COPS

erodes his own credibility and places himself in jeopardy of being blamed for that which he could not prevent from happening. Thus, it is impossible for an effective school administrator to hope to achieve anything in terms of improving the efficiency and effectiveness of the educational process. All he can hope to do is simply give away the store in a cautious manner over the longest period of time possible. Eventually the gang will control the entire system including the board and the finances. The effective administrator simply sets his goal as he enters the system as trying to maintain harmony in the process of giving away the system to the gang. In other words, if he can at least keep the teachers major attention focused upon the education process instead of robbing the board, administration, and taxpayers, then he has sacrificed something of significance out of the ultimate self-destruction of the system. The effective administrator uses a combination of the law, finance, his knowledge of religion, general public opinion, politics, gang fighting instincts, and basic alley knowledge to survive in the process of destruction. He attempts to keep the board informed of legal changes which reduce the power of the gang, even though he knows that they will never be enforced. He tries to bolster board confidence in the path of righteousness in the pursuit of the welfare of the system knowing that all of his efforts at the same time are being undermined by infiltration and insecurity among the board. He realizes that ultimately he will sacrifice himself in an effort to satisfy the system, but in knowing that, maintains the right to choose the time, the place and the issue. Internally the knowledgeable board members realize that the administrator will be sacrificed. Gang members, always ready to sacrifice the novice administrator for any occasion, watch with ridicule and apprehension. Board members with sympathy and compassion allow the administrator to find a new position or a soft place to land. Administrators fight the raging furious battle and struggle toward resistance in all directions knowing that even if they are the last soldiers to stand on the field, ultimately they will lose the war.

In effect, it is impossible for boards of education to police teachers organizations. They do not possess categorically the expertise and experience in all fields of education necessary to separate the accurate legitimate programs proposed by teachers organizations from the irrelevant, shoddy, creative efforts to improve education which cost tax dollars to implement. Board members are forced to try to educate themselves in a quick process of limited exposure to many types of knowledge relating to the educational field. They cannot be expected to become expert in all areas of educational excellence in the short period of time needed before major decisions are thrust upon them. On the other hand, it is natural not to completely trust professionals. The professional is his own worst enemy in that his lack of accuracy or effectiveness destroys and undermines others confidence in him. It is impossible to be perfect. Thus, the administrator, although trained efficient and effective, wise and experienced, gradually makes errors. Who can separate the errors which are truly the result of his own making and those which are forced upon him through political manipulation within the system? In the end analysis, does it matter? He will take responsibility for all of the mistakes which happen under his authority. The fact that he accepts that responsibility will ultimately undermine his image. Once the image is destroyed his position and influence in the community is sure to follow. Such is the destiny accepted by the modern administrator. However, the destiny of the system and the children is that which is truly important. Since the administrator is destroyed by the system he serves, so are the children destroyed by the system that they depend upon. The board bogged down with political upheaval within the system, threats of teacher strikes, lack of funds, public dissent, strive to maintain a consistent, peaceful, prudent position in the maze of destruction. It is impossible for them to always make wise decisions. Ultimately they will be replaced and their successors will be no more equipped nor better able to contend with the decisions than they are. The system simply cannot police itself. There is no way visible upon the immediate horizon to control the gang. The problem is apparent and the results are destroying the system. But no hope is in sight. All those involved realize that the gang is more than a match for both the administrative and the political structure of the system. Taxpayers rage on because the cost of education is skyrocketing. Children complain because the quality of education in the classroom is diminishing. There is resentment toward education and those who perpetuate it, yet there is no hope that the board nor the administration can once again rule the reins controlling the system. It is out of control and beyond recapture. The robbery is in process and the robbers are too strong to be denied.

CHAPTER IX

THE DISCOVERY

The dawn of a new age is upon us. With the failure of tax levies to support the schools and the cry of strikers on the front pages of newspapers, gradually the tip of the iceberg of dissention within the ranks of educators is being discovered. It is logical to assume that the robbery could not continue indefinitely without being discovered by the victims. Such is the case in education today. Gradually parents and children are realizing the shortcomings of the instructional program. Gradually the gang is making slight miscalculations in judgement which expose the true purpose to the public.

In our society we have always respected the teacher as a dedicated, resourceful, public servant. We have looked to our experiences in education as a necessary and essential part of our growth into

THE DISCOVERY

productive citizens. When we see educators degrading their own position in society by standing in picket lines and protesting against the constituency that they are supposed to serve, we realize that something has changed. As we look deeper into the purpose of their behavior, we find that the same dedicated traditional educator that we conceive as a teacher no longer exists. In his place is a modernistic, aggressive, politically dominated individual interested in maintaining and selling the traditional image of education to the taxpaying public.

With this realization comes the inevitable conclusion that teachers no longer see themselves as special nor dedicated. They see themselves as educated labor striving for the same position in our society held by other non-public workers. Teachers no longer want to hold a privileged position of dedication in the image that they portray. Instead they want to be thought of as expensive labor demanding privileged working conditions and situations within the society. As the discovery unfolds, we realize that the new educator thinks of himself as part of the labor force. And with all laborers without dedication, he sees his job as an imposition upon his time and his efforts as beyond what should be expected. When the modern gang member wakes up in the morning, he sees himself as earning a salary for a certain number of hours of exposure to students during the day. This is a very cold unrealistic image for an educator who is expected to lead a child through the developmental stages of his life. He sees himself as struggling to survive in an age of change. As the public discovers this new image, it hardens its opinion toward the process of education. No longer does the public sympathize with the educator who lacks dedication and involvement with his students. The public realizes that in order to develop a young mind in a constructive meaningful manner that that individual must have not only a dedicated resourceful teacher, but also a warm human being with leadership qualities to follow. As the public sees more and more that the type of qualities which attract the new educator are not compatible with the responsibilities of good teaching, the discovery unfolds. The image of teacher versus board of education gradually develops into the image of

THE DISCOVERY

labor versus management. In order for management to survive, it must control labor. As the battle rages for control and the concept of education is lost, the public hardens its views toward the educational process. More and more the cry is heard that children aren't learning, more and more the opinion is heard that parents are dissatisfied with the schools. Daily the schools are charged with wasting resources and materials. News releases cite statistics on learning and show the relationship between the success of students under the old traditional dedicated teachers and the success of students under the modern working gang member. Daily we hear increased teacher complaint.

Traditionally it was unfashionable for a teacher to complain since this detracted from that teacher's dedicated image. However, today it is both fashionable, acceptable, and expected for teachers to complain about all of the factors surrounding their positions of responsibility.

As the discovery continues, the public is outraged. Outraged at the waste of economic resources taking place in the schools. Outraged that their children are not receiving an adequate education. Outraged at the image the new liberal teacher conveys to the public. Outraged that dedication and sincerity are no longer traits to be found in the schools. The public is outraged at the entire system of education.

They fear for their children's future. They fear for the future of the country. They realize that as the educational process disintegrates, so does the country. They realize that education cannot take place without discipline in the classroom. They understand that discipline in the classroom begins with discipline within the teacher. That self-control and self-discipline are traits which are learned through exposure to good examples. They realize that if teachers do not provide the traditional example of self-discipline and dedication to purpose, that students will not learn how to be productive dedicated citizens. They realize that the real value of education is not the knowledge conveyed in the classroom by one person to another, but moreover, the total psychological approach to life that one individual is exposed to during the complete process of education.

More and more the public looks to

THE DISCOVERY

the private sector for answers. As the new buzz words of education lack meaning and significance, mothers look to churches and church schools for guidance. The frills of education are no longer attractive to the tax burdened parent. As they witness their children growing without discipline and direction with little hope for improvement as they develop, they start to look for alternative methods to educate their children. Private schools emerge and private financing follows. Some parents request that tax monies be refunded so that they may invest those funds in schools which are productive. Traditional dedicated educators form small private schools to provide children with the education they need. The public system weakens more. Taxpayers gradually revolt against requests for additional funds. Levies are defeated time and time again forcing the schools into greater debt. As the discovery continues, the public schools can no longer afford to update textbooks as they should. Materials and teaching supplies become obsolete and out of date. This further downgrades the instructional program and emphasizes the ineffectiveness of the system. Questions are raised concerning wasted finances and tax dollars. Answers are not available and instead more educational jargon is manipulated with hope of influencing a discouraged public into further tax support of the schools.

The discovery is at hand. All those involved realize that the schools are failing to meet the needs of public education. Discipline is provided through private and church schools. Moral direction and the image of dedication and tradition is developed on a smallest scale by independent educators. The true professional educators desert the schools in favor of lower salaries, poor working conditions, but a dedication to traditional learning. Private schools attract the traditional dedicated teacher and the public schools are left with the modern worker concept of teacher. The gangs realize that gradually their position is eroding. The public is discovering exactly what the schools are and how they operate. The gang is fearful that discovery will gradually erode their power position. Frantically they try to redevelop public confidence in education. They seek out within their ranks those few educators with their reputations still intact and try to promote their image throughout the community. Hopefully one more time they can pass a tax levy and waste a few more dollars before the final note sounds.

As the discovery develops, the cry for accountability is heard. The taxpayers want the school systems to be accountable for both dollars spent and programs presented. No longer is the taxpaying public willing to accept popular jargon and faddish educational buzz words as the justification for increased expenditures. No longer are taxpayers willing to elect school board members who hire teachers and administrators who are not accountable for their actions. The taxpaying public is interested in how dollars are spent and what results they receive from those expenditures. They want value for their money. They want educational programs that help children learn. In a period of hyperinflation and shrinking dollars, the taxpaying public knows that if the school systems are to survive, they must start to produce efficient cost effective programs that educate children. Along these lines the public looks for cost efficient education. They want to know how much it costs to teach a child mathematics in the first grade or English in the second grade or science in the twelfth grade. They no longer are willing to take the word of vested interest groups in the school system for instructional priorities. They want to be able to dictate through their elected representatives exactly the types of educational programs and philosophy that their dollars will perpetuate. The epitaph of educational revival is prevelant and popular. The discovery demands leadership from both school board members and administrators alike. People want to know that education is taking place and that the results of the efforts being financed are significant. They want their children to learn basic reading, writing and arithmetic and be able to use those skills effectively as responsible citizens.

The discovery process has exposed the educational system for the sham that it is. It has exposed the educators who take advantage of the system as goldbricks of society. It has exposed administrators and inefficient, ineffective board members as responsible for the ruination of the public confidence in education. Along these lines it is necessary to realize that the public is aware of the realities of inefficiency exposed within the system.

Effectiveness and efficiency are no longer popular slogans to be listened to and passed off lightly. The public is now demanding that systems develop effective efficient programs of instruction which prepare children for the future that they are faced with. Times of uncertainty and instability demand that the youth of America be prepared for the challenge ahead. Children realize the system is not taking care of their needs. Students realize that teachers are running popularity contests designed for their own personal benefit. Students want to learn. Students want teachers to present subject matter in an acceptable format which is effective and efficient so that they can prepare themselves for the future ahead. Parents and taxpayers alike are tired of funding gimmick education. They want stability, they want solidity in the system. Demands on the system are great during this period of discovery. Revitalization of education is now the ultimate goal. Throw out the corrupt and the ineffective. Replace them with the efficient, sincere and dedicated teachers who possess the true traditional image of complete education. Select only those educators who are willing to sacrifice through their own dedication in order to satisfy the needs of the students and the public they serve. Rid out the gang members who thrive as leeches upon the system. Weed out the leadership which strives to undermine a system designed to serve the nation. Replace these individuals with demanding, efficient, disciplined educators who desire total commitment on the part of the system for children.

Revitalization of the various instincts which develop a true sincere philosophy of education are needed. The discovery demands that confidence be restored in the system. Taxpayers and parents want to believe that their children are receiving an adequate education. However, in order to believe this they must be convinced through the results of the system. Children must prove to their parents they are learning by demonstrating acceptable knowledge levels and behavioral patterns as a result of exposure to the educational process. No longer will parents believe educators in spite of the actions of their children. The proof is in the pudding, this becomes the byword of proven results.

THE DISCOVERY

Everyone wants the system to succeed. However, success must be proven and not sold to the taxpaying public. No longer will public relations programs designed to convince taxpayers that they are receiving something for their hard earned dollars be enough. From this point forward the public will demand to see the results of the dollars spent.

During this period of discovery those educators who have taken advantage of the system will be forced to pay the price. The inefficient, ineffective gang members who have designed systems to take advantage of the funds available for public education, will now be called forth to answer for their wrongdoing. The price of their behavior has been the gradual development of disrespect for the total educational system. It will be a long hard road to once again reinstate confidence in both the system and the individuals involved. This is the task ahead. And this is the task which is being demanded of both the public and the students. No longer will it be enough to say that a good job is being done. Educators must prove that a good job is being done through the visible results in the behavioral patterns of the students they teach. Better tests will need to be constructed to evaluate student progress. Test results will be made public so the taxpayers can once again develop confidence in the system that they finance. The true credibility of the system is found in the product that it produces. In education that product is an educated student. In order for the system to regain credibility during the discovery period, it is necessary that students demonstrate that they have in fact learned subject matter and are prepared to use that subject matter in a constructive way as productive citizens. This proof will be difficult to visualize unless educators with self-discipline and dedication work together in a systematic way to develop a system which will focus on the ability to display knowledge which has been learned. The public is once again becoming the watchdog of the system. No longer do they have confidence that board members can do the job alone. No longer do they have confidence that administrators based upon their knowledge of education can alone control the system. The public will move in and force the system to be honest, effective, and efficient in carrying out the educational process.

THE DISCOVERY

Once confidence has been regained the system can move on to revitalize the total educational process. The public will demand that there is a revival of the traditional values in education. The crusade will be carried out by those dedicated educators who understand the public demands. The total revival of education is upon us. It is the natural result of the public discovering the ineffectiveness of the present system. It is the natural conclusion for a disheartened public to want the traditional values of what was once an effective educational system to be revitalized and once again effective in producing competent citizens. The revival of education is upon us and those who participate will be the master of their own destiny. Those who resist will perish with the ineffective, inefficient programs that they developed and perpetuated under their own system of self-destruction. All will be held accountable for resources expended in the cause of education. All will be held accountable for programs developed for the future benefit of students. All will be held accountable for every cent expended in the future of education. Justice will be swift and the revival of accountability in education will be quick. Once again respect for the traditional dedicated educator will be the order of the day. Once again the educator who strives for perfection in the classroom and is unselfish in his devotion to his duty will be rewarded. Once again the teacher who cares about children and what they learn can hold his head high and operate in a free system according to his ability and interest. No longer will the educational system be stifled by the gang mentality which has strangled the efforts of traditional dedicated educators. No longer will children be robbed of their right to an education in a free system. No longer will parents and taxpayers be expected to finance an inefficient, ineffective system of education. No longer will anyone be expected to accept for granted that a good job is being done when in fact nothing is being done. Once again the public will be able to have confidence and respect for a system which is serving them in an effective manner. Once again educators will become the pillars of our society. Once again we can count on the strength of an educational system to solve our future problems and lead our country to future successes.

THE DISCOVERY

The discovery will return confidence in the system and once again reward the dedicated traditional educator. The revival, revitalization, and restructuring of education will save the system.

CHAPTER X

THE PUNISHMENT

After a crime is committed there is always punishment. The situation is no different with public education. The gang has committed a crime in robbing the children of their rightful education under a free enterprise system. In order to pay for that crime, both the gang and the system are punished. The gradual erosion of the system which eventually destroys the effectiveness of the teaching process is the first level of punishment. Gradually the system no longer exists. It is ineffective in solving the educational problems of the country.

The taxpaying public has lost its greatest asset. Gradually there is a class distinction in education. People who can afford to send their children to private schools will. If a voucher system is enacted which will allow people to choose

THE PUNISHMENT

between private and public education, the masses will move into private schools. This in effect will leave public education with those children from unfortunate economic circumstances who have no alternative but to participate in a weakened public system. The voucher system would allow the average family to use their real tax dollars for education in a way that they choose. Private schools would bloom throughout the country. A new age in education would develop.

Since the public system is in the process of being destroyed by the gang, it is inevitable that people will look to another source for public education. It's possible that the system could be saved. But in order to save the system from damage that the gang has caused, a complete revival of the traditional values of education are needed. In order to develop a revival of the magnitude which could reverse the current destruction of the educational system, it would be necessary to have a dynamic leader who both understood education and the pitfalls of the past as well as was able to develop continuity with the present process in such a way as to gain the support of those dedicated educators still involved in public education. Thus far, no such person has surfaced as a one and only respected leader in education throughout the country. Unless such an individual surfaces within the next four or five years, the system will be truly lost. So much erosion has occurred and so much damage has been done to the internal structure of education, that it will be virtually impossible to repair and revive the system according to traditional values and ethics.

Thus, it is almost the conclusion that the system will be replaced by another system which is more effective and more efficient and which places the student and the values of learning above the demands and the pressures of a political organization. This system will develop out of the present chaos which makes up the major part of our public educational system. The strength of the system will lie in the private religious schools which will gradually dominate the educational process. The churches have already taken great strides toward developing elementary and secondary schools which serve their constituency on a denominational basis. These schools will grow in size and

THE PUNISHMENT

influence. People will be satisfied with the values being taught since they will be values tied to their religious beliefs. The public schools will be thought of as civil schools, not involved in religion nor ethical principle. They will be thought as the alternative for the weak, the poor, and the unconcerned. The religious schools will gradually develop the reputation of effective, efficient learning processes combined with ethical and religious values. The general result of the religious school process will be a new generation of citizens who will be biased in their values according to the religious teachings they have been exposed to. This could change the entire basic concept of living within the United States. As these new citizens graduate from their religious teachings and take positions of leadership and responsibility in the society, they will bring with them into those positions values and ethics learned on a denominational basis through their education. These new values will then lead businesses and public service occupations into new directions in terms of serving the needs of society. There will be competition between the religions to produce the leaders of tomorrow. As leaders are chosen which possess religious values according to denominational teachings, there would become conflict of new pressure groups and new constituencies within the society.

At the same time, stronger controls will be mandated over the private sector of education. There will be more accountability in all areas of education. Educators will be both required to present curricular patterns which satisfy the academic needs of students as well as provide efficient and effective methods of implementing new curriculum programs. The recruitment of teachers will no longer be a routine nor a politically influenced process. Instead teachers will be selected on the basis of their academic knowledge, achievement, and ability to teach within the classroom. New screening procedures will be developed. Teachers will be hired on a trial basis and student feedback will be used to evaluate the process in the classroom. Once again administrators will be in a position to effectively evaluate classroom performance of the teacher. The evaluation will be strong and often. As a result, weak, ineffective teachers will be eliminated from the system. Once the

THE PUNISHMENT

teacher is selected, there will be programs developed which will help that teacher improve his classroom performance. Programs will be developed which will assist the teacher in developing a stronger knowledge of the subject matter that they are teaching. Old dismissal patterns will be revived, allowing the administration of the new private schools to dismiss those teachers who do not satisfy the demands of the system. Strong evaluation processes will be developed for the entire system and periodically the public paying for religious education will demand accountable measures be applied to the results of the system they are financing. The new private schools will develop adequate teaching pupil ratios. This new relationship will allow teachers both the freedom to work with students individually, as well as the strength of a strong discipline system throughout the school. Citizens will be better informed about what they receive for their dollar paid for education. They will be given periodical reports on the progress of students in a manner that they can understand. The national norms will be abolished. They will be replaced by practical, realistic evaluation procedures which a common ordinary person can interpret and apply. Thus forcing the curricular process to produce knowledge in the form of learning, and share that knowledge with an individual in such a manner that it improves his ability to participate in the society. There will be fewer and weaker contracts between boards of education and teaching groups. Schools will remain small. This will allow the administrations of the various denominational groups to remain in control. A small number of students and a small number of teachers is much easier to manage and satisfy than a large organization with loose controls.

There will be more and closer accountability required over the funds allocated to the educational process. Purchase orders will be scrutinized and curriculums will be developed which do not require the frills in education. All of the busy work which now occupies most of the students' time will be eliminated. There will be a reduction of the social role of the new school. Many of the athletic and extra-curricular programs which are now offered by the public schools will be replaced with instructional programs designed to develop a student's intellectual ability. As a result, the curricular programs will be replaced with social behavioral patterns conducive to the age groups of the students involved. With the heavier work loads and heavier academic responsibilities, students will have less free time for the development of their personality and their personal social preferences.

As a result of the new demands placed upon the private schools, the teachers will be better prepared. Colleges and universities will develop better teacher training programs. These programs will be developed in a rigid manner with discipline at the core. As a result, teachers will come to the classroom better prepared to handle the new values expected from them. Gradually, legislation will require stiffer controls over teacher certification. Teachers will no longer be certified as a result of a minimal college preparatory program. They will be required to serve internships and prove their ability to communicate knowledge in the classroom. As a result, there will be fewer teachers graduating and more demand for good teachers within the system. As demand increases, so will the salary of the teachers who qualify to satisfy the positions within the schools. This will be another technique used to weed out the poor from the effective. Stronger legal controls over expenditures within the schools at all levels will be developed. This will be especially true of the private sector. Since religious organizations are traditionally conservative in their spending patterns, so will they be conservative in their development of private education. For all practical purposes, the gang's influence will be completely abolished. No longer will the gang have a power base which is strong enough to demand negotiation of the basic integral factors of education.

With the small private school taking on the responsibilities of education in the U.S., there will be no need for centralized control. As a result of the strong local control over small school units, it will be virtually impossible to organize the staff of those schools into a coalition with the commonality necessary to once again undermine the educational process. This new small private school concept will allow for the development of varied and diversified ethical standards throughout the system. It will also allow the individual parent and child to choose that particular set of responsibilities and biases which they feel make an adequate educational system.

Thus, instead of a total revival of education throughout the U.S., we will have thousands of mini revivals of value systems throughout the individual communities which make up the country. We will have developing once again thousands of small schools at the same time teaching in general the same basic subject matter but specifically different values, religious concepts and beliefs as part of the ordinary curriculum. These small units will be efficient and effective in terms of controlling the staff and evaluating the instructional process. There will be some hardships in terms of curriculum development. Since it is impossible for a small unit to offer the diverse variety of subjects which can be developed in a larger institution. However, creative curriculum development and creative application of teaching talent will allow the schools to develop well-rounded programs which offer curriculum choices diverse enough to satisfy the demands of the particular student body involved.

This new concept of education will

not be a return to the one room school. Although it seems as if education is moving backwards in terms of growth and development, in reality it is becoming more sophisticated, more specialized, and more effective in terms of satisfying the educational requirements of a diversified citizenry. This can be accomplished through the close control and cooperation of a small group of dedicated educators within a small efficient institutional arrangement. The church school is not a new concept, but it is a new concept for national education. There will be failures among these new schools. However, the success rate will far outweigh the failure rate, and in comparison to the achievement which is now taking place within the public schools, the church schools will appear to be a saving grace. As a result, the schools will develop and flourish with success. As the word spreads that they are doing the job which is needed in education, more and more taxpayers will demand that they be allowed to participate in the private programs. Their demand will eventually lead to legislation which will allow them to use their tax dollars toward education in a school of their choice. Thus, the financial burden of paying both taxes and tuition for a private school will be lifted. The religious organizations which are sponsoring the schools will also develop lobbying campaigns directed toward this end. Once the financial process has been completed which will allow the taxpaying public to legally divert their taxes toward a private school of their choice, the total revolution in education will be at hand. Gradually fewer and fewer students will attend the public schools. Gradually the dedicated sincere teachers now teaching in the public schools will move to the private sector. Thus, public education will be a skeleton of ineffective educators teaching students whose parents are unconcerned. It will gradually wither on the vine. We will see the day when large public institutions with previous enrollment of two and three thousand will literally be empty. Gradually as the private schools develop a stronger base of operation and prove their worth in terms of developing instructional programs, they will become strong enough to come back into the public sector and purchase those empty buildings. Once the private schools are in control of the public buildings and transplant their newly developed instructional programs combined with efficient and effective management of the institutions, the revolution will be complete. A complete revival of education throughout the U.S. will have destroyed the gang and its cancerous influence upon the public resources of education. It will be apparent to all that the gang had truly destroyed itself.

The punishment for undermining education will be self-destruction. The gang will lose all of the power which it has worked so hard to garner. The leaders will fall by the wayside and appear small and insignificant in the shadow of the new religious crusaders in education. Their calls for more money and less teaching time will fall upon silent ears of dedicated educators. Never again will the true professional teacher place monetary gains and material rewards above the satisfaction derived from passing knowledge from one individual to another. Once again teachers will be rewarded by seeing the fruits of their labor go out and produce in a healthy society. Once again educators will occupy a position of respect and sincerity within the society. The mechanical organizational-oriented teacher will be obsolete and removed from the educational scene.

New accounting systems and means for developing effective educational programs will be the rewards of those who survive. As the current political cancer is destroyed within the educational process, the true dedicated professional will surface and be paid for his dedication. Those in charge will recognize both the significance and importance of educators who care about students. They will reward this concern adequately. It will not be necessary to organize for the purpose of political pressure directed toward salary and fringe benefits. True, ethical, dedicated leaders in education will recognize the worth of a disciplined traditional teacher. That teacher in turn will receive the reward which he has coming for the efforts that he contributes to the development of our society.

Thus with the gang approaching the pinnacle of its strength within the current process, we must wait until the erosion weakens the system to the point that the system sub-divides in order to survive. As the subdivision gradually increases and the system becomes totally fragmented, survival will be apparent. That survival will allow the growth and development of the new system. The new order of education will rise out of the dust of destruction of the gang. The punishment of the gang will be the deprivation of involvement in the new order. Thus, those who sold education to the undeserving, will be rewarded with denial of participation in the new system. Accountability and credibility will be the theme song for the new order of dedicated professionals willing to take on the responsibility of preparing the nation's youth for the future. This group will unselfishly develop a curriculum which will prepare students for a challenging future as well as develop a strong moral value system to guide them through the unclear choices ahead. These educators will base their curriculum upon a firm foundation of proven ideals which have withstood the test of time. At the same time, the now sheltered politically-oriented gang will reap the dismal disgust of an awakened nation. Thus, the death of the gang will be the birth of a new era in educational development. The revolution of the taxpaying public against the cancerous effect of the gang will be the beginning of the development of a new educational social order.

Of course it is possible that the dedicated educators who continue to hold the traditional concepts and values of education sacred, will rise up and reevaluate the total position of the system. If these dedicated educators could find the power within the ranks to cleanse education of the cancerous growth of unionism, then it would be possible for them to save the present system without the uncomfortable transition through the private sector. Current statistics indicate that enrollment in private primary and secondary schools has doubled since 1968. Today, nearly one million students attend private schools, only half that number were enrolled ten years ago. At this rate of growth, within the next ten years the public system of education as we know it, will be totally redeveloped. One can ask what causes such a crisis in an institution seemingly as solid as free públic education. We can only look to the pressures which have developed within the society for the solution. We live in a time of economic chaos, a time when people are unsure of the future. This insecurity breeds a natural desire to find protection. The protection that is offered is in the form of gang membership. Thus, the gang has a natural market for its philosophy. In such unsure times filled with insecurity and skepticism about the future, the economy, and the nation as a whole, it is only realistic that people who pride themselves as intellectuals would seek a haven for their discontent. If there are a majority of dedicated educators still functioning within the system, then let them rise up and force the leaders of their organizations to meet the needs of the nation without starving the system that supports them. Let them come out of the classrooms and elect leaders who will carry forth the traditional ideals of the system. Let them prove once again their dedication to not only students and the system but to their individual personal ideals. If it is possible to avoid a revival of educational idealism, then it must be done by each and every dedicated teacher who is willing to step forth and place his own conscience and pride before his paycheck. If individuals of that character exist within the system today, then it is possible to avoid a complete turmoil in national education. However, the momentum is in favor of the revolution. The momentum has reached a proportion where it would take a literal avalanche of personal revelation to reverse the trend which is sweeping the nation. As individual taxpayers, we can do little in this struggle of forces but record the events and react to the issues. We are in the precarious position of paying the bill while at the same time watching the funds being wasted. Change is inevitable and change is in progress. Change does not necessarily mean improvement. In the case of public education, change means self destruction.

CUSTOM HOUSE PRESS
2900 Newark Road
P. O. Box 2369
Zanesville, Ohio 43701

NAME _____

ADDRESS _____

CITY_____ STATE_____ ZIP_____

To Order copies of "THE CHILDREN ROBBERS"

No. of copies_____.

Send name and address and number of copies to above address. Phone orders accepted. Phone (614) 452-7554

_____ PAYMENT ENCLOSED

_____ PLEASE CHARGE TO:

_____ MASTER CHARGE

_____ VISA

_____
Card Number

_____
Expiration Date

_____
Signature

Price - 1 - 50 Copies - $3.75
       50 - 150 Copies - $3.25
       200 - over   - $3.00
(Price includes postage)